Moving On

I0543430

Jacky Warwicker

First published in 2025 by Blossom Spring Publishing
Moving On Copyright © 2025 Jacky Warwicker
ISBN 978-1-917938-02-0
E: admin@blossomspringpublishing.com
W: www.blossomspringpublishing.com
All rights reserved under International Copyright Law.
Contents and/or cover may not be reproduced in whole
or in part without the express written consent of the publisher.
Names, characters, places and incidents are either products of the
author's imagination or are used fictitiously.

For Mum and Dad, part of an inspiring generation.

Chapter 1

'I've joined a Coffin Club,' Jeannie announced as she dried her hands on a tea towel.

'And what do you do there?' Ruth asked with a racing heart.

'I have a cup of tea and a chat with the girls, and then I decorate my coffin.'

'Let me guess, it's purple, with a goat painted on it.'

'Absolutely right, a golden goat climbing a hill,' Jeannie said.

Ruth wondered if this was a preamble to her mother disclosing some devastating news.

'Ted Nugent's ashes got delivered in a box by DPD, and I don't want that happening to me,' Jeannie said.

'Poor Norah, imagine receiving your husband's ashes in the post with the junk mail.'

'It's all she ever talks about these days; it's clearly dementing her.'

'Ted wanted a no-fuss funeral, but he should have considered Norah's needs.'

'What a macabre business, encouraging people to bypass their funeral.'

'People lined the streets and doffed their caps when your grandad's coffin passed by. After the wake, my brothers poured a pint of Guinness over his grave.'

'A filial act of love, good for them.'

'I didn't think the vicar captured the essence of your dad at his funeral,' Jeannie said. 'All that formality and ritual squeezed the life out of him.'

Ruth grimaced at the strangeness of her mother's comment. 'Although Dad's funeral wasn't like Shane MacGowan's, with dancing in the isles, it was beautiful,' she said.

'The vicar drenched the service in platitudes. I could have done a better job myself.'

'Which is why you've joined the Coffin Club - you want a more colourful send-off.'

'Absolutely,' Jeannie said. 'Tell everyone to wear purple to brighten up the solemnity.'

'Trust me, there'll be reverence and revelry at your wake.'

'You don't need to be pop royalty to go out in style,' Jeannie said with a twinkle in her eye.

Ruth started to unpack the shopping as she spoke: 'Jack's calling around later with a ticket for his school play. He's playing Donald in *Blue Remembered Hills*.'

'I can't go,' Jeannie said abruptly.

'What do you mean, you can't go? You always see Jack in his school play, you're his biggest fan.'

'I mean, I can't go and see that particular play - it upsets me too much.'

'That's surprising, you've always loved a good tragedy.'

Jeannie, who had remained upbeat whilst planning her own funeral, began to tremble like a cornered animal. 'If you don't mind, I don't want to talk about it,' she said before scurrying out of the kitchen.

Thinking about the play, Ruth shoved a bag of pasta into the overstocked fridge. *Donald's death in a blazing barn is disturbing, but Mum enjoys intense drama,* she told herself.

In a panicky frame of mind, Ruth reached for her phone and googled: "The early signs of dementia." She scrolled through the list of telling symptoms, until "mood changes" caused her to pause. "We all become moody from time to time. The difference with Alzheimer's is that your loved one can show rapid mood swings from calm to tears to anger, for no apparent reason," she read.

To Ruth's amazement, Jeannie came into the kitchen carrying a small leather suitcase in her hand.

'Are you going somewhere, Mum? You look like Paddington Bear about to leave the jungle of Peru'

'Sadly, my travelling days are over. I just want to look at some old photos from way back.'

'What a lovely idea! You and Dad were such a photogenic couple.'

'The photos in the suitcase were taken when I was an

evacuee,' Jeannie said. 'I haven't looked at them in years.'

In a lightbulb moment, Ruth remembered that her mother was billeted in the Forest of Dean as a child. Curiously, the mention of the play set in the same location had distressed her.

Ruth seized the opportunity to broach the subject: 'Did you enjoy your time as an evacuee, Mum?' she asked.

Jeannie spoke in a faltering voice: 'It was the best of times and the worst of times.'

'Would you like me to look at the photos with you?'

'No, sweetheart. Visiting the past is something I want to do alone. There are key events I need to get clear in my head.'

'Fair enough, I'll tell Jack to call round another day.'

'Does Jack get bullied because he's gay?' Jeannie asked in a concerned voice.

'I know he gets imbecilic comments thrown at him, but Jack's happy in his own skin. He's proud to be gay and doesn't try to hide it.'

'I'm pleased times have changed,' Jeannie said. 'I wish it had been like that in my day.'

'You'll love Jack's new boyfriend. He's bright and stylish, with a thoughtful nature.'

'Just like my grandson,' Jeannie said. 'Tell Jack I'm sorry I can't see his school play.'

'Are you sure you'll be alright, Mum? It isn't always wise to dredge up the past.'

'At my age, you can't shake off the past. Some days it's more vivid than the present.'

Ruth gave her mother a tight hug. 'Ring me if you want some emotional support. And good for you, joining the Coffin Club,' she said.

Clutching the leather suitcase in one hand, Jeannie waved a vigorous goodbye to her daughter. Only when Ruth pulled away in her campervan, did she allow herself to cry.

Chapter 2

Jeannie wiped the suitcase clean before prising it open. The sight of the photos, stacked together in an ad hoc way, caused her to gasp for breath. She shifted them around with one hand as if preparing for a tarot reading.

It lifted Jeannie's heart to see the picture of her and Margot arriving in the Forest of Dean. Dressed in identical berets and belted gaberdines, they looked like inseparable twins bent on adventure.

From the suitcase, Jeannie retrieved a photo of Rita, absorbedly painting at her easel. With her cascading auburn hair and serene face, she had the beauty of an alluring goddess. Drifting back in time, Jeannie recalled the momentous day she met Rita for the first time.

Jeannie stood next to Micky in a long line of jittery evacuees, clutching their gas masks.

Rita arrived late and parked her pram, bursting with canvases, at the back of the room. Dressed like a scarecrow, in an oversized farmer's coat, she joined the villagers perusing the children. When she came to Jeannie, she tilted her head as if studying a piece of art. 'I love your purple ribbon,' she said. 'Did your mummy tie it in your hair?'

'I do my hair myself; I'm a big girl now.'

'Well, you've done a good job. It looks lovely.'

'Purple's my favourite colour.'

'Mine too!' Rita exclaimed. 'Would you like to stay with me in my cottage?'

'Do you have any animals?' Jeannie asked earnestly.

'Just a whippet who likes to snuggle up on my lap.'

'That sounds wonderful. A dog is a man's best friend.'

Rita laughed heartily. 'A girl who speaks freely, you're the one for me.'

Jeannie froze in terror when she saw the cottage at the edge of the woods. It reminded her of a fairytale home of a wicked witch, waiting for a child to gobble up.

'I know you're used to a bustling city,' Rita said, 'but you'll soon come to love the countryside.'

Jeannie looked at the dark, oppressive trees, towering all around her. 'Where are the streets to play in?' she asked.

'Children 'round here play in the woods,' Rita said as she opened the cottage door.

A sleek, black and white whippet ran manically around her mistress before jumping up to lick Jeannie's face. 'I think I'm going to like it here after all,' she said in a fit of giggles.

With a sense of trepidation, Jeannie rummaged around and took a photo from the bottom of the suitcase.

Fortuitously, it was another reminder of the blissful days she'd spent in the Forest of Dean. In the photo, she was blithely painting a tree, with the whippet by her side.

Although it was a sepia image, she recalled using an array of bright colours in the style of Matisse. Rita had shown her pictures of the artist's work and encouraged her to be playful in her painting. 'That's amazing, angel,' she heard Rita say. 'You're a born artist.'

How many people help mould us into who we become? Jeannie asked herself. *Rita was a pivotal person in my life, she lit a flame within me.*

Intent on retrieving her precious memories from the past, Jeannie pushed the suitcase aside and leant back in her chair. Within minutes, she'd scrambled past the murder to the time when she was a sprightly evacuee in the Forest of Dean.

Chapter 3

Jeannie bristled with pride as she pushed the pram, bulging with pots and pans, to the recycling depot. She marvelled that the metal would be used to help build the ships and aeroplanes needed in the war.

'I'm doing my bit to fight the enemy,' she told Micky when she met him in the street.

'Wow, I can't believe you've collected so much,' he said, full of admiration. 'Do you want my help?'

'Yes, please. My arms are beginning to ache, I could do with a rest.'

Micky, with his frail body, struggled to push the pram up the inclining path. Embarrassed on his behalf, Jeannie suggested they push it together.

'My mum visited yesterday,' she told Micky. 'I overheard her talking to Rita about the Germans bombing Bristol. She said the mediaeval part of the city was a raging inferno.'

'That's awful, we'll never see it again.'

'Mum said, "A thousand years of heritage perished in one night."'

'A church shelter in my gran's street got blown to pieces.'

Drowning out Jeannie's reply, Simon shouted from his bicycle: 'Squeaky, squeaky Micky Mouse, pushing a girl's pram. Wait 'til I tell the others.'

'Tell them what?' Jeannie snapped. 'That he's helping the war effort?'

Micky dropped his head and muttered something inaudible under his breath.

Jeannie wished she had a superpower and could topple Simon off his bicycle. 'He's a right arse,' she said.

'What does that mean?' Micky asked with genuine interest.

'I don't know but it sounds good.'

'Aye, it does,' Micky agreed. 'Have we much further to go?'

'No, the depot's at the top of the hill. Let's go and see the snowdrops before we push on.'

They put the break on the pram and raced to see the cluster of white flowers peppering the grass. The snowdrops pushed up through the earth like miniature candles on a forest green carpet. On their knees, the children examined the wondrous flowers growing in the gloom of winter.

'I wish I was strong like the snowdrops, then my dad wouldn't call me "weedy",' Micky said.

'Take no notice of him, you're extra special. None of the other boys would help me push the pram.'

'I don't know what I'd do without you, Jeannie. No one else talks to me.'

'At least you're staying with a big family. There's only me and Rita in the cottage.'

'What's it like, living there?' Micky asked, staring intently into Jeannie's eyes.

'Oh, it's great. Rita makes everything such fun; I don't even mind the toilet being halfway up the garden.'

Micky fell silent and waited for Jeannie to continue.

'When Rita feeds the hens, she greets them by name and trills along to their clucking. At breakfast, we dunk soldiers into runny eggs and make up stories about the hens of Gloucestershire.'

'Lucky you, I'm not allowed to join in with the Frasers. After I've finished chopping the wood, I'm sent to the scullery to eat one slice of bread and lard. Whenever the family go out, Mr Fraser locks me in my bedroom.'

'Oh, Micky, that's dreadful,' Jeannie said.

'What upsets me most, is that Mr Fraser keeps the money and parcels my mum sends.'

'Write to your family, let them know what's happening.'

'I do, but Mr Fraser checks my letters and makes me change the bits he doesn't like.'

'Rita will rescue you from that wicked bully,' Jeannie said, blazing with confidence. 'Come on, Micky, let's deliver the pots and pans as fast as we can.'

Jeannie left the pram in the yard and ran into the cottage to tell Rita her pressing news.

Just as she hoped, Rita sprang into action immediately. 'Micky's not staying another night in that godforsaken place. Keep your coat on, Jeannie, we've got work to do.'

Her gaberdine flapping in the wind, Rita charged like an intrepid superhero to Fraser's farm.

Sensing the urgency, Jeannie ran faster than she'd ever done before to keep abreast. She imagined Rita doing sharp karate chops before kicking down Micky's bedroom door.

The sight of his solitary figure, raking leaves in the garden, brought Jeannie back to reality.

Micky startled like a frightened rabbit at the sound of their gravelly footsteps.

'We've come to rescue you,' Jeannie called out to assuage his fear.

Micky glanced at the house and stood rigidly still as if he'd been turned to stone.

Jeannie saw Fraser step menacingly onto the porch. 'Quick, Micky, get away!' she urged in a desperate voice.

'We've come to get the boy, you've been treating him like an animal,' Rita told the tyrannical host.

'You're the mad artist everyone talks about, get off my land,' Fraser called out in anger. Riled up like a bull, he strode in Micky's direction with a look of fury on his face.

'Fraser's coming to get you! Run, Micky, run,' Jeannie yelled.

Alerted to the fast-approaching despot, Micky screwed up his courage and bolted towards her.

Jeannie grasped him in her arms. 'You're safe, Micky,' she cried in relief. 'No one can hurt you now.'

Chapter 4

Rita pounded the dolly peg in a large tub of boiling water to clean the soiled sheet.

'Why does Micky keep wetting the bed?' Jeannie asked in a concerned voice.

'The poor boy's not sleeping properly. Micky has nightmares about being locked in his bedroom at Fraser's farm.'

'I'll take him into the woods to play. That will lift his spirits.'

Rita smiled at Jeannie's choice of words. 'That's a good idea,' she said as she twisted the dripping wet sheet with her hands.

Jeannie watched keenly as Rita rotated the cast iron mangle to complete the morning ritual. To her amusement, the bedding got squeezed so tight, it emerged like a plank of ice.

'How would you like to see a play?' Rita asked. 'The Osiris Players are performing *She Stoops to Conquer* in the village hall. It's one of my favourite comedies; I saw it when I was a girl.'

Jeannie jumped up and down on the spot. 'Oh, Rita, that sounds amazing. Will Micky be coming with us?'

'Of course, a dose of laughter will cheer him up.'

'He'll be so excited when I tell him.'

Despite Jeannie's ebullience, Micky was adamant that he didn't want to see the play.

'It's a comedy, Micky, you'll love it,' Jeannie said.

'Mr Fraser might be there,' he stammered.

Rita spoke in a soothing voice: 'Forget about him. You should never have been billeted with that awful man.'

Jeannie put the ticket for *She Stoops to Conquer* in Micky's hand. 'I'll be there to protect you,' she said. 'Don't let the bullies get you down.'

The village hall crackled with energy as people took their seats to see the play.

Jeannie waited with her mouth wide open for The Osiris Players to start their performance. Rita whispered that they were Britain's first all-female professional theatre company, adding to the allure.

Throughout the production, Jeannie watched mesmerised, as seven women transformed themselves into eighteenth-century beauties, foppish beaux and thigh-slapping squires. The actors flipping between identities bewitched her with their rollicking antics and unbridled gusto.

At the end of the play, Jeannie ran outside to speak to the mercurial players. Starstruck, she saw them loading up the horse and dray with scenery and eye-catching costumes.

Impulsively, Jeannie darted up to a dark-haired woman streaked in greasepaint.

'Can I come with you on your tour?' she asked.

The actor spoke seriously: 'You're too young at the moment, but one day, maybe.'

One day, Jeannie promised herself, as the company rode jubilantly into the distance.

By the time Jeannie returned to the hall, Micky was curled up in his seat, struggling to breathe. Fraser loomed over him, prodding his back with a loathsome grimace on his face.

Jeannie crept up behind the sly bully and kicked him hard in the shin.

Fraser whirled around to confront his assailant and grabbed her by the wrist.

Jeannie winced in pain before hurling herself into a theatrical performance to attract attention. 'Help! Help! He's hurting me!' she howled melodramatically, like a skilled player.

Incensed, Rita stormed across the room. 'Let her go, you brute,' she hollered, to the delight of the disbanding audience. Emulating a combative knight, she stabbed the sharp tip of her umbrella into Fraser's wobbly belly.

Racing to get away, he caught his foot on the refreshment table and toppled forwards.

A large jug of milk crashed down on top of Fraser's prostrate body, soaking his shirt.

The villagers laughed uproariously as he staggered

sheepishly towards the door.

Jeannie ran over to comfort Micky, but he too was chortling at Fraser's spectacular downfall.

Chapter 5

Jeannie stopped to admire the mass of double white hawthorn blossoms adorning the woods. 'The trees look like they're going to a wedding,' she said, full of delight.

Micky picked up a sprig of blossom from the ground and handed it to her. 'Put it in your hair, you'll look like a bridesmaid.'

Jeannie sniffed the scent of the star-shaped flowers before placing it behind her ear. 'Rita says there's going to be Maypole dancing on the green,' she said.

'Can the boys join in?' Micky asked eagerly.

'Oh, yes, it's great fun. I'll show you how to do it.'

Jeannie reached out and took Micky's hand. 'You take four steps towards the Maypole, four steps back and circle for eight,' she instructed.

'I love dancing, but my dad says it's only for girls.'

Simon jumped out from behind a tree. 'It is Micky Mouse. You won't catch me doing it.'

'Clear off, you're spoiling our fun,' Jeannie said firmly.

'You're both nuts,' Simon taunted as he hurled a stone in their direction.

'Haven't you got anything better to do with your time than bullying others?' Jeannie asked in a disdainful tone.

'I'm off to build a shelter in the woods for the gang to

hide in. There's an escaped   Italian on the loose, and he's got a long knife.'

'You're just making it up to frighten us,' Micky said.

'I don't need to do that; you're frightened of your own shadows.'

'Watch out, Simon! I can see the prisoner of war behind you,' Jeannie shouted out.

'Ain't no Italian getting me,' Simon screamed, as he bolted through the bracken like a startled goose.

He's getting closer,' Jeannie yelled to ratchet up the drama. Eyes aglow, she turned to Micky. 'Imagine tying that peabrain to the Maypole and dancing around him.'

'We could plait the ribbons tighter and tighter, until he agrees to join in.'

Jeannie suddenly put her finger to her lips to silence Micky. 'Look at that beautiful green bird in the hawthorn tree,' she whispered.

The children crept closer to scrutinise the bold yellow stripes above the bird's eyes. They saw its lemon-white chest quiver as it warbled a melancholic song of falling notes.

Unsettled by the sad sound piercing the silence, Micky shuffled his feet back and forth. 'Do you like living in the country?' he asked.

'I love it. Rita says I've become "a child of nature."'

'She's gone to paint the Italian prisoner of war, who's

working on Blackett's farm.'

'Rita's doing a series of paintings depicting wartime Britain,' Jeannie said, using the words she'd read in the newspaper.

'Do you think we could meet the Italian?'

'What if he stabs us with his pitchfork?'

'The Italian prisoners of war are just ordinary men serving their country, like your dad.'

Jeannie thought of her father, miles from home doing his bit for King and Country. 'Let's escape the gang and go up to Blackett's farm,' she said.

Rita had stopped painting by the time the children reached the golden wheat field.

Observing her deep in conversation with the Italian, Jeannie pulled Micky back from intruding on their privacy.

When Rita noticed the hovering children, she broke off talking to the prisoner of war and waved them over. In her usual upbeat voice, she introduced the handsome Italian as her friend.

Gino ruffled Micky's hair as if he'd known him for a long time. 'I have a brother about your age who lives in Naples,' he said in a faltering voice.

Rita looked at Gino attentively, prompting him to continue: 'I long to hear how my family is doing, but there is no news. War feels like an endless tunnel from which there is no escape.'

'Keep hope in your heart, Gino; the wretched war will end one day,' Rita said soothingly.

Chapter 6

Jeannie looked at the slivers of light streaming across the open suitcase. *You've retrieved happy memories so far, leave it there*, she warned herself.

Unable to resist the strong pull of the past, she reached for another wartime photo. It was a snapshot of Rita, heavily pregnant, with a radiant smile on her face. Snippets of gossip came back to Jeannie:

'An Italian prisoner of war's the father, little hussy.'

'She's been out dancing with the black G.I.s, what a tart.'

Jeannie shuffled the photos in the suitcase around until she found one of the gang, The Foresters. She scrutinised the innocent-looking children in home-knitted jumpers with a pounding heart. Four winsome members of the gang looked incapable of cruelty and spite. The fifth, Simon, leant forward with tightly clenched fists, as if spoiling for a fight.

Jeannie saw herself with the purple ribbon on top of her hair, holding an upside-down doll by one leg. Micky, by her side, had a blanket in his hand and was sucking his thumb. Margot's head was turned fully to the right, as if something had caught her attention.

Jeannie dropped the photo. Memories of Micky's appalling death assailed her with sickening clarity.

Harry burst through the bushes and aimed a bow and arrow directly at Andrew. 'Why didn't you wait for me? I told you I wanted to be in the photo.'

Simon dived at Harry's feet and wrestled him to the ground. 'Say sorry to the girls for frightening them.'

'Harry's just a great pretender,' Margot said. 'No one's scared of him.'

'Squeaky, squeaky, Micky Mouse is, look at him trembling,' Simon sneered.

'Leave him alone, he helps me with the war effort,' Jeannie snapped.

'Pushing a pram full of pots and pans, he's just a big girl.'

'Take no notice of him, Micky, he's a loser. Come on, let's go and see Gino.'

'The Italian prisoner of war, who works on the farm?' Andrew asked. 'What do you want to be friends with him for?'

'Gino tells us great stories about his family in Naples,' Jeannie replied.

'I hope they get bombed to death,' Simon said viciously.

'Be careful what you say,' Margot told him. 'It could be your family that gets blown to pieces.'

Micky waited until he was away from the gang to wrap the blanket around Jeannie's doll. Cradling it in his arms, he sang a sweet lullaby as they strolled to Blackett's farm.

Behind Rita's abandoned easel, the golden yellow wheat shone in the sunlight. Jeannie expected to see the handsome Italian working in the fields, but he was nowhere in sight.

Micky plonked himself down on the grass and placed the doll on his lap.

Jeannie sat cross-legged by his side. 'I'm chewing the cud,' she said.

'Does it taste nice?'

'You say the funniest things, Micky. What bothers me is that Rita's cleared away her paints but left the easel - she never does that.'

'Perhaps she's gone for a walk with Gino.'

Jeannie looked all around the verdant farmland. 'They're nowhere to be seen, that's for sure,' she said.

'They could be having a lie down in the barn,' Micky suggested. 'Shall we go and see?'

'I don't want to wake them up, let's go to the waterfall instead.'

'Is your dad a nice man?' Micky asked as they entered the ancient forest.

'He's the best,' Jeannie said. 'I'm praying he doesn't get killed in the war.'

'I bet he doesn't beat you with a belt to get the devil

24

out of you.'

'Of course not, he sits me on his lap and makes up the most brilliant stories.'

'My dad says he's ashamed that I'm not like other boys.'

'You're special, Micky, and I like you just the way you are,' Jeannie said in a tender voice.

Chapter 7

Jeannie pulled her face in disgust as she inhaled the pungent smell of wood garlic. On the forest bank, swathes of pine green leaves curled around intensely white flowers.

'Rita's going to make some wild garlic and nettle soup,' Jeannie told Micky.

'Perhaps she'll make some for Gino.'

'I wish I was old enough to drink Rita's elderflower wine.'

'My mum never drinks alcohol; she's seen what it does to my dad.'

'We've been walking for ages, how far is the waterfall?'

'There are so many paths, I can't remember,' Micky replied.

'Hush, listen to that gushing sound. I think we're close.'

'I can hear voices; do you think it could be the gang?'

'No, they're building a den over by the bridge.'

'I'm hot,' Micky said, wiping the sweat from his brow.

'Take off your top, that will help you cool down.'

'I don't like showing my body, it's too scrawny.'

'Who's told you that?' Jeannie asked. 'Your dad?'

Micky was about to answer when the fast, cascading water came into view. In full flow, the falls thundered over the rocks with mighty force into the river.

Jeannie stared at the spectacle with her mouth wide open. 'Wow!' she exclaimed.

'If I could swim, I'd dive into that beautiful river,' Micky said.

Jeannie scrambled out of her dress and threw it to the ground.

'Just come for a paddle,' she called out before plunging into the shiny water.

In heavenly bliss, Jeannie lay on her back, with her face bathed in sunlight. Entering a trance-like state, she closed her eyes and let the rolling river carry her downstream.

The sound of shrill, excited voices, overlapping in a frenzy, caused Jeannie to panic. She dipped under the water and lost control before pushing upward into the breaststroke.

Despite her effort to gain speed, Jeannie's limbs tired against the downward current of the water. 'Keep on going,' she urged herself as she endeavoured to swim back to Micky.

Bleary-eyed on the bank, she saw some children in the distance dragging a girl to the waterfall. They laughed and cheered as they ducked her under the crashing water.

Jeannie ignored the mayhem and ran in the opposite direction to look for Micky.

Perturbed that she couldn't find him, Jeannie hollered his name in her loudest voice. When Micky didn't reply, she began retracing her steps in search of distinct landmarks.

Jeannie saw her doll wrapped in the blanket, wedged between two mossy rocks. It was the exact spot where she'd whipped off her dress and thrown it to the ground.

Jeannie looked towards the waterfall where the children were packed together like a savage beast. 'Oh my God!' she screamed. 'It isn't a girl being ducked in the water; it's Micky wearing my dress.'

Pumped with adrenaline, Jeannie pelted along the riverbank to rescue him.

Chapter 8

Jeannie saw the gang scrambling over slimy boulders as she neared the waterfall.

Only Simon remained in the water, holding Micky like a dangling puppet.

Andrew turned to look at the unfolding scene before bolting into the forest. The others followed him swiftly, with their heads hung low.

Simon scowled as he dragged Micky's frail body through the deepening water.

Jeannie raced forward until she reached the stony bank immediately above them. 'Micky can't swim,' she yelled in alarm.

Simon caught her eye. 'Good,' he called back.

Micky screamed as Simon grabbed him with two hands and yanked him into the air.

Her panic rising, Jeannie ran too fast down the bank and lost her footing.

Flat on the ground, she heard Simon cry out: 'I hope you drown in your girly dress.'

Despite her pain, Jeannie jumped to her feet and saw him hurling Micky into the fast-flowing river.

'He's going under,' Simon shouted with glee.

Jeannie watched, rigid with fright, as Micky frantically thrashed his arms around. His little head bobbed above the water and then, in a split second, he was gone.

'Micky's drowning, you've got to rescue him,' Jeannie hollered.

Hearing her plea, Simon swam quickly in Micky's direction and plunged into the water.

Jeannie clasped her hands tightly together. 'Please, God, let him find Micky,' she said, over and over.

When Simon resurfaced, gasping for breath, Jeannie saw the petrified look on his face. 'You've got to keep searching for Micky,' she shouted in a distraught voice.

Mustering his courage, Simon swam further downstream and dived into the perilous river.

Jeannie stared intently at the water as she raced along the bank trying to locate his whereabouts.

'No! No!' she wailed pitifully when Simon reemerged empty-handed from the river.

Wretched and shivering, he cried out in desperation: 'I can't find Micky.'

Jeannie screamed from the bank: 'You threw him into the water! You're a murderer, Simon.'

'Micky was dancing around in your dress,' he muttered, clambering out of the river.

Full of uncontrollable rage, Jeannie rushed forward to attack the monstrous boy. Intent on hurting him, she clawed viciously at his ashen face.

Simon pushed her away. 'It was only a game,' he said pathetically.

Unsteady on her feet, Jeannie saw the red-hot fear in his eyes before she crashed to the ground.

Distressed by the memory, Jeannie let an immense wave of grief wash over her.

Poor, poor Micky. What a tragic waste of life, she lamented.

Anxious to lock the past away, Jeannie placed the group photo face down in the suitcase.

'Don't be rash, savour what was special about Micky,' she heard Frank say.

Instantly, Jeannie pictured Micky dancing in the woods with a beatific smile on his face. No longer drowning in the river, her brilliant friend was full of zest and energy. *That's how I'll remember Micky*, Jeannie told herself as she closed the suitcase.

Seeing her shift in the chair, the dog leapt out of her basket and began to whine.

To pacify her faithful companion, Jeannie stroked the whippet gently on the chest. 'Come on, old girl, let's get some fresh air,' she said briskly to liven up her mood.

In the garden, Jeannie admired the beauty of Frank's work. Tall, bearded irises brushed against the sundial; red velvety snapdragons ran the length of the stone wall.

Everything was carefully planned to create an oasis of wonder. She thought forlornly about the house viewings and the trail of strangers traipsing into their sanctuary.

'Oh, Frank,' Jeannie cried, 'I don't want a new beginning in some strange place.'

'No one's making you move, my lovely,' she heard him say. 'Stay in the house, if you want to.'

'Being here without you is too painful. I thought a fresh start might do me good.'

'Take it easy,' Frank said. 'Remember what I told you about riding the Wind Horse through the turbulence of life.'

Trying to be composed, Jeannie recalled her husband's guiding words: 'Imagine a horse galloping through a beautiful meadow, feel that life force running through you.'

'It's impossible without you, Frank,' Jeannie said. 'I don't even have the courage to go to Jack's play.'

Chapter 9

Jeannie was putting on her coat to go to the Coffin Club when her phone rang.

'Hi, Mum. How are you feeling this morning?' Ruth asked in a perky voice.

'A little better, now I've decided not to sell the house.'

'That's news, I thought you were set on moving?'

'It just doesn't feel right, sweetheart. I need to get back on the horse.'

Ruth laughed like an amused parent. 'Whatever you decide to do is the right thing,' she said.

'Paul McCartney's playing at The Echo Arena, I thought Jack might like to go with me.'

'I'll ask him. He's keen to give you a ticket for *Blue Remembered Hills*.'

'Have you told Jack I don't want to see the play?'

'No, I was hoping you'd change your mind.'

'Well, I haven't. It would be too much for me.'

'How did you get on looking at the photos yesterday?' Ruth asked, probingly.

'It was distressing at times, but I retrieved some lovely memories.'

'I'm surprised you haven't talked more about your days as an evacuee.'

'I told your dad all about Rita, she made such an

impact on my life.'

'I'll take you to the Forest of Dean if you ever want to revisit.'

'There was a terrific scandal about the birth of Rita's baby, but she was fiercely proud of her son.'

'I'm sorry, Mum, there's someone knocking at the door. I'll ring you back later.'

'Bye-bye,' Jeannie said, overlapping Ruth's goodbye.

The sun pouring into the living room illuminated a thick layer of dust on the sideboard. Jeannie drew a sad face on top of it with her fingertip before fastening her coat.

Noticing the time, she picked up the cake for the Coffin Club members and rushed through the door.

'I love that golden goat,' Elsie said, 'it looks like it's climbing the stairway to heaven.'

'It beats a boring brown coffin, that's for sure,' Jeannie said.

'Thanks for the cake. I'm afraid baking's not my forte. I once made a quiche, and my daughter asked if there was any more "biscuit."'

'No one's good at everything. We all have our talents.'

'You've got more than one, your coffin looks like a real work of art.'

'Painting's been one of my passions since I was a girl.'

'Do you need help undoing that water bottle?' Elsie asked.

'Yes, please. I really struggle opening things these days.'

'I'll send you a link to the "Manage at Home" website. They've got loads of useful gadgets for people with weak hands.'

'I feel like I've lost my right arm without Frank around,' Jeannie said wistfully.

'Billy was a lazy sod, but he knew how to put a smile on my face.'

'That counts for a lot. It's the companionable silences I miss.'

'Well, here comes a bloke who can talk for England,' Elsie whispered.

Jeannie's heart sank, Gerald was the one person in the Coffin Club she didn't like. Loud and opinionated, even at his old age he couldn't talk to women without trying to flirt with them. She picked up her brush and, in the style of Van Gogh, began painting swirls of deep blue on the side of the coffin.

As luck would have it, Gerald didn't even stop to speak to them and headed straight to the bathroom.

Jeannie seized the opportunity to immerse herself fully in her labour of love. Using layers of vivid colour, she painted an inky night, bedecked with bright yellow stars on the wooden panel.

Jeannie remembered being in the Forest of Dean on such a wondrous night. Rita stooped down beside her and pointed at the brightest star. 'That's Micky, shining in the sky,' she said, in a voice full of awe.

Chapter 10

Jeannie sat in the chair that overlooked the front garden, shaded by a misshaped conifer tree. She felt an affinity with the needleless branches of the evergreen, which clung to the craggy trunk. Withered on one side, yet rich in foliage on the other, the conifer had two distinct halves. *Just like me*, Jeannie thought, *stunted by age but soldiering on.*

Even though it wasn't cold, she placed the mauve throw which Frank had given her, over her lap. 'Something to keep you warm,' Jeannie heard him say in his jovial voice. Today, she was using his gift as a comfort blanket to help her feel secure.

Jeannie sifted through the suitcase looking for a photo of Rita's baby. Unexpectedly, she came across a flimsy, yellow letter from her mother. Keeping her emotions in check, she put on her glasses to read the faded words:

Dear sweetheart,

It was wonderful spending time with you at the weekend. I can't believe how you've grown since you left home. Being in the countryside and eating all those vegetables suits you.

Darling, I know Micky's death was a great shock and

has broken your heart. It's so sad that such a sweet, kind boy died in an accident. I'm pleased you had a good cry and told me all about him.

What a blessing that you're staying with someone as lovely as Rita. Daddy and I feel that our prayers have been answered. There's intensive bombing in Bristol, and it's comforting to know you're safe in the Forest of Dean.

Thank you for your fabulous painting of the dancer. I've put it in a frame and hung it in the kitchen. Grandma and Grandad loved your story about the girl who made the onion cry. Keep writing and painting, Jeannie, it helps lift the spirits.

One day, when the war is over, we'll all be together again. Until then, do what makes you happy and be a good girl for Rita.

Lots of love,
Mummy and Daddy

My poor parents, having to send their only child away from home, was Jeannie's immediate thought. She imagined waving goodbye to Ruth at a railway station in a war-ravaged city, to fully comprehend their pain.

It was a great blessing for us all that I was billeted with Rita, Jeannie told herself. Intent on replaying the time with her joyous host, she closed her eyes and drifted back to the past.

With a critical eye, Rita arranged her paintings along the garden wall. 'Pick your favourite, Jeannie, and tell me why you like it,' she said.

A striking image of Gino, stacking the hay with his strong, muscular arms, caught Jeannie's attention. She was drawn to the look of absorption on his face and the raven blackness of his hair.

Aware that Rita was watching her like a proud parent, Jeannie scrutinised all the paintings with great care. The other prisoners of war working on the farm looked plain next to Gino. He alone had dark, sparkly eyes and a bewitching smile.

Jeannie pointed to the painting of Gino sitting merrily on a bright yellow tractor. 'This is my favourite,' she said, 'because Gino reminds me of a handsome prince on a throne.'

'I'll miss him when he goes home to Italy,' Rita said. 'Maybe we could both visit him in Naples.'

'Will we still be friends when the war ends?' Jeannie asked.

'Of course,' Rita said, 'you will always have a special place in my heart.'

'I'm not friends with Simon anymore,' Jeannie confessed. 'He deliberately threw Micky into the water; I saw him do it.'

'The police said it was an accident, sweetheart. Simon told them he was trying to rescue Micky.'

'When I'm older, I'll let everyone know that Simon's a murderer.'

'You're upset at the moment, Jeannie, but your anger will pass.'

'I've promised Micky it won't, until people know the truth.'

Rita furrowed her brows but spoke in a lively voice: 'Do you want to come and walk the dog with me? A bit of exercise will do us both the world of good.'

Chapter 11

Jeannie looked at the fabrics in the shop with knots in her stomach.

'Let me know if you see anything you like,' Rita said kindly.

Jeannie didn't want a new summer dress; she wanted her old one back, and Micky still to be alive.

'How about this?' Rita asked, pointing to an apple-green fabric, dotted with flowers.

Uncharacteristically, Jeannie struggled to speak. She wanted to say, 'Simon really did murder, Micky, but instead, she examined the cloth with feigned interest.

'It's fine,' Jeannie eventually said, in a cheerless voice.

'That's not the answer I was looking for,' Rita told her. 'Let's keep searching until you find something you love. We need to use your mum's coupons wisely.'

This registered with Jeannie and she forced the image of Micky, drowning in her dress, out of her head. In its place, she pictured the vibrant colours favoured by Rita - magenta, blood orange, sapphire blue.

A smart-looking assistant with short wavy hair stepped over to them. 'Can I help you with anything?' she asked efficiently.

'Jeannie's got an eye for colour, I'm letting her choose

the fabric,' Rita said with a smile.

Buoyed up by the compliment, Jeannie looked in earnest for some striking material. 'Oh, this is gorgeous,' she said, pointing to a purple fabric with shimmering gold stars.

'That will make such a pretty dress!' Rita exclaimed. 'You can wear it when your mum comes to visit.'

'She'll be thrilled that we've used the coupons wisely,' Jeannie said.

In a happy frame of mind, Rita stopped to admire the photographs on display in a shop window. Black men with big beaming smiles on their faces were throwing their dance partners into the air.

'That looks more fun than Maypole dancing,' Jeannie remarked.

'They're doing the jitterbug,' Rita said, 'it's all the rage on the dance floors.'

'I'll show you how to boogie,' an American soldier said cockily over her shoulder. 'Don't get dancing with any black trash, you'll get yourself a bad name.'

'Keep your racist comments to yourself; I'll dance with whom I want to,' Rita said sharply.

With her head held high, she grabbed Jeannie's hand, and together they marched up the street.

Jeannie was sure the handsome soldier coming towards them was one of the men she'd seen in the photographs. Before she could mention this to Rita, the white soldier spurted past them like a charging bull.

In full daylight, he ran up to the black man and punched him hard in the face several times. With his hand covered in blood, the vicious attacker yelled: 'Leave the white girls alone, you raping bastard. Next time you'll get lynched.'

Rita screamed out in alarm before running to the aid of the injured soldier. 'Are you alright?' she asked with genuine concern.

'I'll recover,' he said bravely. 'It's not the first time I've been attacked in the street.'

Rita took off one of her cotton gloves. 'Use this to soak up the blood,' she urged.

'You must be my dame in shining armour,' the American said in a smoky voice.

Rita laughed, despite the severity of the situation. 'Come home with me, and I'll put some ointment on your cuts,' she said.

'That's a great idea,' Jeannie interjected. 'Then, when you're better, you can teach us how to jitterbug.'

'It must be my lucky day after all,' the soldier said, looking at Rita.

Chapter 12

When Leon came out of the bathroom, Rita examined his face like an attentive nurse. 'A few nasty cuts, but hopefully, they'll heal soon,' she said.

'No racist white man's gonna stop me from dancing,' Leon stated.

Jeannie took the fabric out of the paper bag and held it in front of her.

Leon whistled from across the room to express his approval. 'My, oh, my, what beautiful material,' he said, bringing a glow to Jeannie's cheeks. 'You English girls sure know how to dress.'

Rita looked at the smart American in his immaculate uniform. 'You look pretty dapper yourself,' she remarked.

"Reminds me of one of my favourite songs,' Leon said. 'Mind if I play it on the piano?'

'Feel free,' Rita said, charmed by his sunshiny confidence.

'It's called *Dapper Dan*; it sounds better with a saxophone, but it's a great tune.' As Leon's fingers slid across the piano, he belted out the song in his strong, jazzy voice.

Jeannie looked at Rita, swaying expressively to the music. 'Can we do the jitterbug?' she asked eagerly.

'We sure can,' Leon replied. 'I'll show you some

single-time swing steps.'

Struck by his easy-going manner, Jeannie thought of Micky being taunted by Simon for wanting to dance.

'Keep your back straight as you move forward and bounce,' Leon instructed. 'Work on getting a break in the pelvis, so you can feel the movement.'

'You make it look so easy,' Rita said, as she clumsily attempted the move.

'Try the step pulse, simply shift your weight from one foot to the other with your knees bent. Step-drop, step-drop - great, Jeannie. Now, incorporate a rock step, make sure you use the ball of your feet as you step back. Lift your knees up towards the rib cage to get the rhythm going.'

'I guess it will be a long time before I hit the dance floor,' Rita said with a giggle.

'You'll be surprised how quickly you pick up the basic steps,' Leon said as he took her hand. 'I'll move to the right, and you go to the left. Let's start with the pulse - step and drop, step and drop. Now, the rock step, keep your front foot flat and step back on the ball of your foot. That's terrific, Rita.'

Jeannie saw the couple's sparkling joy as they boogied together. Swept up by their merriment, she clapped vigorously to encourage them.

Micky would have loved the jitterbug, Jeannie said to

herself. *I wish he was here to dance with me.* Before Rita could see her crying, she raced into the kitchen to be alone.

Sitting bleary-eyed at the table, Jeannie looked at her painting of the tulips. It pleased her that the vibrant orange, dashed with red, captured the gaiety of the flowers. *My mum will love the painting,* she thought with a surge of pride. *I'll put it in the post for her birthday.*

The catchy sound of jazz being played on the piano made Jeannie leap to her feet. Putting down her glass, she noticed a white envelope addressed to Gino on the windowsill. Rita had written his name artistically, in fancy, curling letters, and added a small heart beneath it.

Jeannie imagined the telling words written in the letter: *Dearest darling Gino, you are my handsome Italian prince, and I long for the war to end so we can be together.*

Flushed with excitement, Rita called out from the doorway: 'Come on, Jeannie, you're missing all the fun. Leon's playing some marvellous music.'

Chapter 13

'It's very high up,' Jeannie said as she climbed into the campervan.

'Who are you visiting first in the Forest of Dean?' Ruth asked before she started the engine.

'Rita's son, Ethan. There was such a hullabaloo when he was born.'

'Why was that, Mum?'

'Because of the colour of his skin and the fact that Rita wasn't married.'

'Were you there when he was born?'

'I was. His father, Leon, was a handsome black G.I., and Rita was passionately in love with him.'

'Why didn't they get married?'

'Because the US military didn't allow black G.I.s to marry white women.'

'Which meant their children were born illegitimate - that's shocking.'

'You've got to remember that in the 1940s, there was still segregation in America.'

'But the black G.I.s were over here as part of the US military, fighting for democracy.'

'It counted for nothing. When the army knew Rita was pregnant, they transferred Leon to another part of the country.'

'Heartbreaking. Sounds like you're going to have an emotional day.'

'I'm looking forward to meeting Ethan, he sounded lovely over the phone.'

'An exciting trip down memory lane,' Ruth said, starting the engine.

Jeannie turned towards the house and pictured Frank in the window, waving her goodbye.

In the ensuing silence, she recalled seeing Ethan wrapped in his mother's loving arms. An adorable brown baby with masses of black hair, he was blissfully asleep.

Rita's farewell words rang in Jeannie's ears: 'Bye, darling. It's been wonderful having you here with me. I will miss our fun times together.'

As if it were yesterday, Jeannie remembered her own parting words: 'I've been the luckiest girl on the planet staying with you.'

'A match made in heaven,' Rita said. 'Make sure you come back to visit us.'

'I feel so bad that this is my first visit to the Forest of Dean since I was an evacuee,' Jeannie told Ruth.

'Don't worry about that, Mum. You'll have a great time meeting Ethan and going to the reunion.'

Jeannie was half-expecting Rita to open the cottage door with a paintbrush in her hand. 'What took you so long?'

she imagined her saying in her soft Gloucestershire brogue. Instead, Ethan, an old man, but unmistakably Rita and Leon's son, greeted her warmly.

Just like his father, he had deep brown eyes, which twinkled when he spoke. 'My mum talked a lot about you and Micky, right up to the end of her life,' Ethan said.

'That's heartwarming,' Jeannie told him, 'Rita was our guiding light during the war years.'

'She was a strong, inspiring woman. I had the best of mothers.'

A dappled ray of sunlight fell across the piano. 'Your father was incredibly charismatic; he swept Rita off her feet.'

'She loved him with a passion all her life, it's a travesty they couldn't get married.'

'Did you get to meet your father? 'Jeannie asked gently.

'Thankfully, I did, but only after my stepfather died,' Ethan said. 'Gino was a wonderful man, and I didn't want to upset him.'

'Rita married Gino?' Jeannie said with a note of incredulity in her voice.

'It's a long story. Can I get you anything to eat or drink before I give you the low-down?'

'Just a glass of water will be fine,' Jeannie said. 'Ethan, don't feel under any pressure to talk about the past.'

'It will be a pleasure sharing my story with you.'

Jeannie watched Ethan go into the kitchen with his head held high. *He's Rita's son alright,* she thought with a surge of love for them both.

Chapter 14

Although the furniture in the living room was different, the comforting atmosphere Jeannie had known as a child remained.

Ethan settled into a velvet armchair near the fireplace. 'My mum and dad were in love, they didn't try to hide their relationship,' he said.

Jeannie sensed Rita in the room, listening attentively to the conversation.

'They got engaged and did everything they could to stay together,' Ethan added.

'My mum even went to Virginia to try to marry my dad, but she got deported back to England.'

'It must have been so hard for Rita,' Jeannie remarked.

'Fortunately, my gran was amazing, which helped my mum weather the storm. Some idiots tormented her by calling out "Nigger lover" and banging dustbin lids when she went by, but mainly the neighbours were supportive.'

'What was it like for you, growing up in such a tight-knit community?'

'People looked out for me; I was the pet of the village.'

'That's great. I encountered a real mix of people when I lived here.'

'Of course, I was subject to name calling: "Blackie",

"Little Chocolate Boy", "Sambo." A teacher even asked me if I wanted to do an African dance in front of the class. But I always felt incredibly loved and part of the community[1].'

'Did Gino stay in the Forest of Dean after the war?' Jeannie asked.

'Yes, he continued to work here so he could marry my mum.'

'Gino was a charming man; I remember him well.'

'He was a very special person; he loved both Mum and me with all his heart.'

'Did Rita stay in touch with Leon after she married Gino?'

'No, all their love letters pre-date the marriage.'

Ethan caught sight of Jeannie shifting in her seat. 'My mum did what was best for me,' he said. 'On her deathbed, she held my dad's photo as a young G.I., but it was Gino who tended her.'

'Did your father keep in touch with you?' Jeannie asked.

Ethan smiled as he spoke: 'All his life, he sent me birthday cards and letters. I wrote back, telling him how I was doing in school and boasting about my athletic prowess.'

---

[1] *Britain's 'Brown Babies'* by Lucy Bland. Published in May 2019 by Manchester University Press.

'Your father was a generous soul,' Jeannie said. 'What was it like, meeting him for the first time?'

'It was the best day of my life. When he held me in his arms, the power of his love shot right through me. I couldn't stop crying.'

'It sounds like a blissful reunion.'

'Everything about it was perfect. Although I'd grown up in a loving family, I always felt like part of me was missing. Being with my dad made me feel whole.'

'Did you get to meet his family and friends?' Jeannie asked.

'I certainly did. Everyone knew he had a son overseas, and they all prayed that one day he would meet me. I was my dad's only child, and they were overjoyed when I visited him.'

'Did you manage to return to America?' Jeannie asked.

'Yes, I went to see my dad as often as I could. It was wonderful being with him, we had so much in common. We both loved poetry, painting and the same type of music.'

'It sounds like you were natural soulmates.'

'Getting to know my dad before he died was an amazing gift. In finding him, I found the other half of myself.'

'What a moving story,' Jeannie remarked.

'It always fills me with pride telling it,' Ethan said. 'Are you visiting anyone else in the Forest of Dean?'

'Tomorrow I'm going to an evacuee reunion in the village hall. There's someone I especially want to see,' Jeannie said.

Chapter 15

Jeannie found it impossible to imagine Simon as an old man, all she could picture was him hurling Micky into the water with a smirk on his face. To dissipate the anger boiling up inside her, she recalled Ethan's infectious joy when he spoke about his dad.

Pleased to see Ruth enjoying afternoon tea on the hotel lawn, Jeannie strode over to join her. 'Hi, sweetheart,' she said, 'those macaroons look amazing.'

'It's a special treat to celebrate you venturing away from home,' Ruth told her.

'I must do it more often, this feels like being on holiday,' Jeannie replied.

'How did it go with Ethan?' Ruth asked as she poured her mother a cup of tea.

'It was an extremely moving visit. Ethan grew up surrounded by love and forged a deep bond with both his parents.'

'I'm pleased that being illegitimate didn't stigmatise his life. It was criminal that the American government forbade black G.I.s to marry white women.'

'Approximately 2,000 brown babies were born in Britain in the Second World War,' Jeannie said. 'More than half of them were put into orphanages or up for adoption.'

'It's great that things worked out for Ethan. How did you feel, stepping back into the cottage?'

'I had a sense of homecoming, as if Rita was still there, waiting for me to return.'

Ruth buttered a scone as she spoke: 'It must have been hard saying goodbye to her after the war. Did Rita stay single all her life?

'No, she married Gino, an Italian prisoner of war.'

'It's such a shame she couldn't marry the father of her son. It must have been heart-wrenching for her.'

'All because of the colour of Leon's skin,' Jeannie said.

'It was easier for Rita to marry a prisoner of war than a black G.I. who was fighting for his country.'

'She got forced into a difficult situation. I chose to end my first relationship, and that was bad enough.'

'Well, that's news to me. How come you've not mentioned this before?'

'No child wants to hear about their mother's love life.'

'Now you've piqued my interest, I'm all ears,' Ruth said, leaning forwards.

'His name was Rowan, and I met him when I was a drama student in Liverpool.'

Jeannie stopped speaking, but the eagerness in Ruth's eyes compelled her to continue: 'He was tall, with curly black hair and sea-green eyes. When I saw him in the rehearsal room for the first time, I felt like he was an old friend from way back.'

'Rowan's a lovely name, was he of Irish descent?'

'Yes, he was. His Irish ancestors arrived in Liverpool at the same time as mine, in the 1840s.'

'Perhaps you knew each other in another life,' Ruth said playfully.

'When Rowan came over to me, there was a spark of recognition in his eyes. I thought he was going to say, "Don't I know you from somewhere?" but instead, he handed me a script.'

'You're making it sound like love at first sight.'

'When I took the script from Rowan's hand, we held each other's gaze for a long while.'

'Why did you break up?' Ruth asked with interest.

'I wanted to find my own way in the world before settling down.'

'Good for you, flying solo takes guts.'

'It was hard letting go of my first love, but at least I didn't have a baby, like Rita.'

'Because of your courage, you ended up with a fulfilling career and a great husband.'

Jeannie sipped on her tea and perused the light blue butterfly, flitting around the peonies.

'I discovered a spectacular waterfall this morning,' Ruth said. 'It's not far from here, you probably know it.'

Aware that her hand was shaking, Jeannie put her cup down on the table. 'I do,' she tried to say, but the painful words stuck in her throat.

Chapter 16

Jeannie hesitated before slipping the electric blue maxi dress off the hanger. Without Frank by her side, she wasn't sure she had the confidence to wear it.

'Come on, my lovely,' she heard him say, 'it's perfect for the reunion.'

Persuaded by Frank's emphatic guidance, Jeannie put on the glamorous dress. Completely transformed by the garment, *Good choice*, she told herself as she did up the zip.

Back in the familiar village hall, a warm feeling of gratitude took Jeannie by surprise. She wanted to be in a pugnacious mood to confront Simon, but instead, loving memories flooded back to her. With childlike excitement, Jeannie recalled the momentous day Rita took her to see *She Stoops to Conquer*. Picturing the merry band of women giving it their all on stage, she said a silent "thank you" to the Osiris Players.

'I thought you'd be wearing something stupendous,' a lady called out from behind her.

When Jeannie turned around, despite the greyness of the lady's hair, Jeannie instantly recognised her childhood friend. 'Margot!' she exclaimed in utter delight. 'I was hoping you would be here.'

'It's wonderful to see you. All the gang have managed

to make it this year.'

'Good job we've got name tags,' Jeannie said, 'at least I'll be able to call everyone by their right name.'

'There are some great photographs of The Foresters on display. Oh, we had such a fun time cavorting in the woods.'

Until Micky's awful death, Jeannie wanted to say. Instead, she linked Margot's arm in a breezy manner to walk over to the wartime exhibits.

'Let's take a trip down memory lane,' Jeannie said in a cheerful voice.

'There's a photo of Rita painting the prisoner of war,' Margot pointed out. 'Did you keep in touch with her after the war?'

'No,' Jeannie said. 'I wanted to, but we moved to Liverpool because of my dad's job.'

Margot looked directly into Jeannie's eyes as if she was expecting her to say more. 'They were difficult years when the war ended, everyone struggled to get by.'

Jeannie heard a gravity in Margot's voice which inferred she had a tale to tell. 'At least we were safe in the Forest of Dean when Bristol was being torn apart,' she said.

'There's you holding your doll,' Margot said, 'with a purple ribbon in your hair.'

Margot failed to say that Micky was by Jeannie's side,

with the blue blanket around his shoulders. Jeannie stared at his coy face, partially hidden by the blonde hair brushing against his eyes. *I haven't forgotten my promise, Micky. I'll let everyone know Simon murdered you*, she vowed.

'"The happy highways where I went and cannot come again,"[2]' Margot said, looking at the photographs.

Jeannie glanced around the room. 'Any idea where we'll find the gang?' she asked.

'Propping up the bar, most likely. Do you fancy a drink?'

'That would be nice, especially if we manage to locate the men.'

Whilst Jeannie was speaking, Margot waved to someone across the room. 'Unless I'm very much mistaken, that's Harry beckoning us over,' she said.

Jeannie remained upbeat and pleasant as they approached the bald-headed men. *Thank God for the labels*, she told herself, *age has altered them out of all recognition.*

'How are our favourite wartime girls?' Harry asked as he rose from his stool to greet them.

'All the better for being reunited with The Foresters,' Margot said.

---

[2] Poem XL from *A Shropshire Lad*, by A.E Housman, originally published in 1896.

'We band of brothers,' Andrew cheered, raising his glass.

Jeannie hugged each man in turn until she came to Simon. Seizing the moment, she stepped back with an audible gasp to attract the gang's attention. When all eyes were fixed on her, Jeannie called out in a loud, compelling voice: 'Simon, the one who murdered Micky for wearing my dress.'

Chapter 17

'You know Micky's death was an accident,' Simon said in a surprisingly steady voice.

'I saw the look of hatred in your eyes when you hurled Micky into the water. You meant to kill him, Simon.'

'Jeannie, you're being theatrical, as always. I did a stupid thing that still haunts me to this day. When I saw Micky in your dress, I wanted to teach him a lesson.'

'Micky was a unique and beautiful soul, what was it you wanted to teach him, Simon? To be a murderer, like you?'

'I was playing around when I threw Micky into the water, I had no intention of drowning him. It was a stupid prank that went wrong.'

'You're distorting the truth; I know for sure you wanted him dead.'

'Then we'll agree to differ,' Simon said, with a misplaced smile that angered Jeannie.

Resisting the temptation to smack him across the face, she controlled her fury and spoke in a plain manner: 'Nothing you say will change my mind. In a fit of rage, you killed Micky because he was different. His innocent blood is on your hands, Simon.'

Paying no heed to the others, Jeannie walked away from the group with an air of defiance.

Outside in the peaceful garden, she looked for the brightest star shining in the sky. 'Everyone in the gang knows Simon's a murderer,' she whispered. 'Rest in peace, Micky.'

Jeannie sat down on a bench to savour the stillness of the velvety night. Her mind turned to Jack's play and the tragedy that befell Donald in the barn. Locked in by the other children, he couldn't escape the blazing fire that engulfed him in flames and claimed his life. *Oh, the cruelty of children*, Jeannie lamented, as a shadowy figure walked towards her.

Margot seemed edgy as she perched on the bench. 'Are you alright?' she asked in a concerned voice.

Jeannie spoke from the heart: 'I will never get over Micky's death, he was like a brother to me.' Although it was dark, she noticed a piteous look of concern fall across Margot's face.

'Jeannie, I'm praying I'm doing the right thing, but I think there's something you should know,' Margot said.

The hooting sound of an owl piercing the silence sent shivers down Jeannie's spine. 'What is it you've been aching to tell me?' she asked.

'You have a half-brother who lives in Bristol,' Margot divulged.

'You're completely mistaken,' Jeannie said swiftly. 'Sadly, I'm an only child.'

'The news came directly from your aunt before she died. She wanted to leave the boy some money and requested help to find him.'

'I can't believe my father had a child I didn't know about.'

'The boy was your mother's son,' Margot said. 'She gave birth to him when you were in the Forest of Dean and your dad was away at war.'

'That's complete nonsense,' Jeannie snapped. 'My mum was devoted to my dad.'

'I don't know the ins and outs of what happened, just that your mum had an illegitimate baby during the war years.'

The sincerity in Margot's voice hit Jeannie hard. 'That's shocking, I had no idea,' she said. 'Was the baby given up for adoption?'

'Yes. And when your dad came home, he got a new job in Liverpool.'

'I can't understand why my dad didn't bring the boy up as his own. Gino was a loving stepfather to Rita's son.'

'His circumstances were different. It was a blessing for you that your parents stayed together.'

'But my mum had to give up her son, it must have been heartbreaking for her.'

'Did you ever suspect you had a half-brother?' Margot asked.

'Honestly, this is complete news to me. My mum and dad kept it a secret from me all their lives.'

'Back then, illegitimacy held a massive stigma. Especially for the women who gave birth whilst their husbands were away at war.'

Jeannie thought of Rita, desperate to keep her beloved son but forced into having an illegitimate child. 'The war's got a lot to answer for,' she said. 'Lives got torn apart in so many ways.'

'I guess you'll be keen to leave after such a traumatic evening.'

'Oh, no,' Jeannie said. 'I haven't come all this way to get an early night. I intend to have a good dance at the reunion, in honour of Micky.'

Pleased to be alone in the hotel garden, Jeannie sat near the apple tree so she could see the birds.

A shiny magpie with purplish-blue wings settled on a low-hanging branch. 'One for sorrow,' Jeannie uttered, as she scanned the sturdy tree for a second bird. To her relief, a second magpie with a magnificent tail was perched on a higher branch. 'Two for joy,' Jeannie said appreciatively, despite her contempt for superstitious people.

After the turmoil of her night, she savoured the fresh morning light heralding a new day. Picking up her pen, Jeannie recalled the weekly ritual of writing to her parents as an evacuee. A time when her letters, detailing the minutiae of life in the Forest of Dean, were the ramblings of a child. Besieged by a gamut of emotions, *It's far more difficult, writing as an adult*, she told herself.

No longer needing to enquire about her parents' health, Jeannie wondered how to begin her letter. Perturbed by the lies surrounding her half-brother's birth, she decided to start on an accusatory note:

Dear Mum and Dad,

Margot's revelation about your shameful secret has left me shattered. You did a great wrong, keeping the truth from me.

In the darkest of times, you were my beacon of light. Today, I must question how much I really knew you.

Without Margot's brave disclosure, I might never have learnt of Charlie's existence. Is that what you really wanted? To deny me the chance to love and cherish my half-brother?

It was cruel of you to oust Charlie from the family home and put him up for adoption. Knowing that you didn't have it in your heart to care for an innocent baby appals me. When I meet Charlie, I will shower him with the love you denied him.

Jeannie wiped away the tears in her eyes with the palm of her hand.

'*Darling,*' she heard her mother say, '*I wanted to keep Charlie more than anything in the world. Do you really think I didn't have it in my heart to love my darling boy? When Daddy came back from the war, he was hurt in so many ways.*

Charlie's presence caused him great distress, and I couldn't bear his suffering. Although it was incredibly painful, I did what was best for all of us. Daddy was a kind and caring man, but he couldn't come to terms with my betrayal. Losing my son was the price I paid for loving two men.'

In a pensive frame of mind, Jeannie turned to a fresh page in her notebook. *Mum, forgive me for judging you*, she wrote. *You were a beautiful soul, and you alone know your truth.*

Jeannie listed a few disjointed words about her father before connecting her thoughts. *Dad, I know you suffered when you came back from the war*, she wrote. *Seeing Uncle Harry blown to pieces in front of you must have been hell on earth. I'm not surprised you needed electric shock treatment and tranquillisers. If you had been well, things might have worked out differently for our family. I'm grateful that you did your best for Mum and me, we were lucky to have you.*

Soothed by her writing, Jeannie sat for a while, taking in the beauty of the garden. Pale yellow roses, tinged with pink, brushed against a sundial; statuesque delphiniums towered regally over the fishpond.

'Mum, Mum,' a voice called out, grabbing Jeannie's attention. To her dismay, she saw Ruth running towards her with an agonised look on her face.

Jeannie stood up, sending her notebook flying to the ground.

Ruth spoke quickly in a panicky voice: 'Jack's gone missing. Tony rang to say he didn't hear from him after they left the club.'

'Perhaps his phone ran out of battery,' Jeannie said, with a pounding heart.

'Jack hasn't turned up for the dress rehearsal of the play. Something's seriously wrong.'

Although her body was trembling, Jeannie spoke in a calm voice: 'We'll find him, sweetheart. Let's pack our bags and go home.'

Chapter 19

Sitting in the van beside her distressed daughter, Jeannie was assailed by a complete feeling of dread. Tangled thoughts relating to Micky's death and Jack's disappearance entwined in her head. She imagined her grandson being attacked in a back alley by a crazy youth, affronted by his sexuality.

Jeannie closed her eyes, hoping to blank out of the nightmare scenario.

'Don't fall asleep,' she heard Frank say. 'You need to be on your mettle for the family.'

Paying heed to his advice, Jeannie sat up straight in her seat as the traffic came to a standstill. 'Do you want me to put some music on?' she said, trying to be helpful.

'Bloody traffic jam,' Ruth cried out, ignoring her question.

'It's only road works,' Jeannie said, 'the traffic's on the move further ahead.'

'I feel it in my bones that something's happened to Jack,' Ruth said in a quavering voice.

'Try to stay strong, angel, we're nearly home now. Do you think we should let Ryan know Jack's gone missing?'

'Absolutely not, that selfish bastard doesn't care about his son,' Ruth snapped.

Rather than add to the palpable tension rising in the van, Jeannie said nothing.

When the road cleared, Ruth put her foot down on the accelerator to make up for lost time. 'Can you check my phone to see if Tony's left a message?' she said over the roar of the engine.

Jeannie realised there had been a missed call whilst they were packing the van. She read Tony's WhatsApp message silently before speaking: 'Jack's been found, sweetheart. He got attacked by a gang of thieves who stole his watch.'

'Oh my God, is he alright?'

'Yes, his dad took him to A&E to get a few stitches. Jack stayed at Ryan's last night.'

'Thank heavens he's not dead,' Ruth said as she pulled into a lay-by. 'Why did Jack ask his dad for help; he hasn't seen him in years?'

Hearing the anguish in Ruth's voice, Jeannie leant over and gave her a tight hug. 'Jack's still alive, that's the important thing,' she said.

'Ryan walked out on me when I had postnatal depression. I don't want him in our lives.'

'Ryan needed treatment for his own postnatal depression. When he was better, you wouldn't have him back.'

'Ryan abandoned me when I needed him the most.'

'It was a traumatic time for both of you.'

'Are you siding with Ryan after all I've been through?'

'No, I'm trying to be fair. It's clear that Jack's been in contact with his dad.'

'All of this went on behind my back, I'm furious.'

'Give Ryan a chance, he is Jack's father, after all.'

'We've managed without him for all these years, he has no right barging back into our lives.'

'You'll need to hear Jack's side of the story,' Jeannie cautioned.

After a stony silence, Ruth spoke in a more conciliatory voice: 'I wonder if Jack managed to make the dress rehearsal.'

'He did. Tony said he got a hero's welcome from the cast when he walked in. Do you mind dropping me off at the school, I can't rest until I've seen Jack.'

'The drama teacher won't let you into the studio,' Ruth stated.

'Marion's a good friend of mine, I'm sure she'll let me have a sneak preview of the play.'

'I thought you didn't want to see *Blue Remembered Hills*.'

'That was before the reunion, things are different now.'

'Jack will be thrilled that you've changed your mind.'

'I want to applaud my wonderful, brave grandson,' Jeannie said. 'He's the light of my life.'

Chapter 20

With Marion's blessing, Jeannie climbed to the top of the raked auditorium to watch the play. A powerful sense of homecoming reminded her of the years she'd spent in the theatre. *Halcyon days of creativity and camaraderie*, Jeannie thought as she pulled down her seat.

She looked admiringly at the set, depicting three distinct places in the Forest of Dean. The stage lights focused on a woodland area where two boys were fighting with pumped-up aggression. As they thumped and clouted each other with increasing vigour, a sprightly group of children called out their names from the sidelines.

Jeannie's eyes were drawn to a young girl holding a chocolate-coloured doll as if it were a real-life baby. Disquieting memories of the riverbank where Micky met his death flashed through her mind.

The sudden sound of a siren blasting from the speakers brought Jeannie back to the present. With precision timing, the startled children froze in their tracks.

'That's from the prisoner-of-war camp! One of them bloody Ities have got loose,'[3] John said cockily.

When the siren escalated in volume, the children raced

---

[3] From here on, all onstage dialogue is from Blue Remembered Hills Acting Edition published by Samuel French on January 1, 1990.

like frightened rabbits along the woodland path.

A pretty girl, pushing a squeaking pram, let out a wail. 'I want to go home! I want to go ho-o-me!' she hollered.

The boy wearing a gun belt with a pistol cried out urgently: 'L-Lul - Listen!'

The cowering children quaked in fear as the sound of screeching birds echoed around them.

In utter panic, the miniature cowboy bolted from the group and ran towards the trees.

The others darted after him at breakneck speed, abandoning the rickety doll's pram on the path.

Jeannie shifted in her seat as the children, gasping and panting, hurtled beast-like through the ferns. Their collective frenzy reminded her of The Foresters cheering and laughing as Simon ducked Micky under the water.

Whilst the children on stage plunged to safety in a hollow, Jeannie pictured Micky in her dress, bobbing up and down like a puppet.

The sight of Peter crashing through the undergrowth with bullish enjoyment heightened her distress.

Relishing his power, the boy jumped forcibly on top of the hollow to terrify the children. 'Frightened, was you?' he called out in a jubilant voice.

'We been bloody crying down in here,' a girl in metal-framed glasses confessed.

Peter's eyes glowed with pleasure. 'Donald Duck is

trembling like a jelly. Him oodn't leave the barn,' he said gleefully.

'The Itie killed two or three guards to get out of the camp. Slit their throats,' John announced to ratchet up the terror.

'What about my poor little Dinah? Her'll cry and cry, and cry,' the pretty girl said with a sob.

As if their fight had never taken place, John addressed Peter in a friendly voice: 'Shall us go and get the pram?'

'Oy. Come on then.'

The boys gave each other a smug look before turning in unison to climb out of the hollow.

In complete silence, the four remaining children huddled together with their eyes tightly closed.

Jeannie admired the smooth lighting transition which illuminated John and Peter creeping comedically through the trees.

In a wicked mood, the boys let out squawky, spine-chilling cries to frighten their companions.

'No-o-o-oo--oo! Aaaaaaah! Him have got me! Aaaaah! The knife!' John shrieked.

'Keep away! Keep away! No-o-o-oo! Aaaaaagh! I be done for!' Peter cried out.

The jubilant boys rolled around the ground, helpless with suppressed laughter.

To Jeannie's dismay, the lights crosscut to the petrified

children shaking in the hollow. Their fear reminded her of Micky's frenzied panic when Simon hurled him into the river.

Above the actors' voices, Jeannie heard Micky's pitiful cry for help crescendo into a blood-curdling scream.

Chapter 21

Jeannie was already crying by the time the lights switched to the barn. Feeling vulnerable, she wanted to rush out of the theatre before the tragic ending of the play. Only the thought of seeing Jack perform gave her the courage to stay.

A tension-filled hush preceded Donald striking matches with childlike fascination.

Jeannie was impressed that her robust, happy-go-lucky grandson looked so frail and intense on stage.

Donald let each match burn down to his fingers before dropping it to the ground. All the time, he glanced around anxiously like a bird fearing attack.

Watching a flame with utter absorption, a new expression flared up in his eyes. Donald turned and stared so intently at a bale of hay that the match burnt his finger. 'Oh!' he cried out as the lights dimmed on the barn.

Jeannie marvelled that Jack was giving such a captivating performance in the wake of the attack. 'He's our brave and talented grandson,' she told Frank with a glow of pride.

Stage left, the lights framed the petrified children huddled in the hollow. They screamed in unified terror as the pram came crashing down on top of them.

Peter and John laughed uproariously at the shocked

faces of their blubbering friends.

Incensed, Audrey scrambled out of the hollow and in a violent fit of temper, knocked Peter to the ground. 'I'll bash you up! Bash you up!' she yelled, pummelling the boy's chest.

Jeannie recalled her own animalistic rage when she attacked Simon on the riverbank.

Peter, making grunting sounds, rolled on top of Audrey and pinned down her arms.

'Look! Look!' Willie called out in alarm. 'It's the Itie! And him have got a gurt long knife!'

Peter jumped up in fear. 'W-where?' he demanded nervously.

'Gotcha! Gotcha!' Willie rejoiced, pumping his fist in the air.

'I shall smack thou one!' Peter said in fury.

'We have made a hell of a racket, ant us?' John declared.

'The Itie might have heard,' Peter said in a serious voice.

Appalled by the idea, the children looked at each other in total dread.

'Come on! I byunt stopping. Let's run for it!' Peter called out.

The others followed swiftly, crashing through the ferns and undergrowth in ragged formation.

Jeannie thought of The Foresters scrambling over the boulders in hot pursuit of Andrew.

A yellow pool of light illuminated Donald stooped in the barn, striking a match. Cupping his hand to shield the flame, he leant forward to ignite a bale of hay.

'Aw, come on. Come on,' he said, his face twitching uncontrollably. A small flame flared and fluttered, before slowly curling along the edges of the hay. Excited by the crackling sound of the fire, Donald did a little dance with his thumb stuck in his mouth.

Full of delight, he picked up some drier hay and held it over the flames. 'Come on, come on, come on,' Donald repeated in a trance-like state.

Although it was make-believe, Jeannie felt the burning heat of the fire as it began to blaze. Distraught on Donald's behalf, she closed her eyes to blot out the tragic scene.

Chapter 22

Jeannie listened carefully to the dialogue leading up to Donald's death.

'Wonder if Donald Duck is still hiding in the barn?' Peter asked.

'Poor old Quack Quack,' Willie said, making the children laugh.

'Let's pretend to be the Italian,' John suggested with a twinkle in his eye.

Peter pounced on the idea: 'Frighten him to death,' he said spitefully.

His pernicious words caused Jeannie to gasp. She pictured herself flat on the ground as Simon called out to Micky: 'I hope you drown in your girlie dress.'

Geed up by the idea of tormenting Donald, the children on stage sizzled with energy. 'Last one to the barn is a cissy!' Peter yelled, inciting them to burst into action.

Jeannie's heartbeat quickened, the unfolding tragedy on stage seemed all too real. For a moment she thought it was Jack admiring the size of the fire he had created. *It's a play*, she told herself in a strict, schoolmarmish voice. *Just a play.*

Donald watched in awe as the flames engulfed a greater mass of hay. His eyes followed the few tongues of fire, stretching up to the roof.

With his mouth wide open, he backed towards the door which was propped open by a stone. 'Burn you bugger! Burn! Burn!' Donald called out in a commanding voice.

The flames seemed to swell and belly out suddenly. Donald scurried away but before he could reach the door, it slammed shut with a bang.

Jeannie heard the children giggle with glee at their escapade. They placed a stone behind the door and held it shut with six pairs of hands.

'Open the door! Help! Help!' Donald hollered to their delight.

Even when the children saw smoke seeping under the door, they shrieked with laughter.

'Open the door! Please! Please! Open the door! Plea-ea-ease!' Donald implored.

Jeannie thought of Micky's harrowing cry for help before he slipped under the water.

In a complete mindless panic, Donald retreated from the door and ran towards a window. The flames crackled around the entrance to the barn, blocking his only exit. He dashed around, screaming, before a roof timber collapsed beside him in a shower of sparks.

Jeannie trembled in her seat as the lights crosscut to the children.

They all had a look of consternation on their faces but Willie was the first to grasp the horror of the situation. 'Quick! Quick!' he shouted out. 'Open the door! Open it!'

'Open it!' Angela yelled at the top of her voice.

In a flustered frenzy, the children dragged open the barn door. Hot, burning flames leapt towards them, into the air.

The children's shrill cries of terror sent shivers down Jeannie's spine. She recalled Simon scrambling from the river with a petrified look on his face. 'I can't find Micky,' he cried out in anguish.

In a heart-rending moment, Jeannie saw Donald gesticulating through the flames before the fire engulfed him.

The distressed children pelted away from the barn into a field of tall grass. Cowering in shame and shock, they sat away from one another whilst the raging fire burned on.

'We don't know nothing about it, do us?' Peter said eagerly.

Jeannie realised it was impossible for the children to face the savage truth. She remembered Simon's denial at the reunion: 'I was playing around when I threw Micky into the water, I didn't mean to drown him. It was a stupid prank that went wrong.'

The sense of compassion Jeannie felt for the guilt-ridden children on stage, deeply unsettled her. *Simon has had to live with the fact that he caused Micky's death*, she told herself.

'Poor old Quack Quack,' Peter said, as the children's haunting sobs echoed around the auditorium.

Chapter 23

When Jack stepped into the auditorium, Jeannie's mouth dropped open in shock.

Thrilled to see his grandma, he embraced her with great warmth and affection. 'Mum texted that you were coming,' he said perkily, despite the lacerations on his face.

Jeannie took Jack's arm and steered him away from the group. In a quiet part of the theatre, she spoke in a soothing voice: 'It looks like someone's given you a real kicking.'

'The attackers stole Grandad's watch,' Jack said, close to tears.

'Don't worry about that. Your being safe is the only thing that matters.'

'After I left Tony, I turned down a back alley, and the gang leapt out at me.'

'Oh, poor you!' Jeannie said. 'It must have been terrifying.'

'It was. There were three muggers, I didn't stand a chance.'

Remembering Audrey in the play, Jeannie pictured herself as Super Gran, bashing up the assailants. 'Have you reported the attack to the police?' she asked.

'Yes. They said there's been a spate of watch thefts in

the area. Apparently, it's a crime that's on the increase.'

'Interesting,' Jeannie said. 'I'll do some sleuthing.'

Jack gave her a quizzical look. 'Don't get doing anything foolish,' he advised. 'These men are lethal criminals.'

'No one beats up my grandson and gets away with it,' Jeannie said.

'Did you like the play?' Jack asked, tactfully changing the subject.

'I loved it. Your performance blew me away. At one point, I forgot I was in theatre, you were so convincing. I almost raced onto the stage to rescue you from the blazing barn. Your grandad would have been so proud of you.'

'Thanks for coming to the dress rehearsal, Grandma,' Jack said. 'You're the one person I wanted to see the play.'

'You were so brave performing after the attack, I wanted to support you.'

'To be quite honest, I didn't feel very well, but I couldn't let the cast down.'

'Do you feel better now?'

'Yes, but I'm looking forward to getting some rest. Does Mum know I've been in touch with my dad?'

'She does,' Jeannie said. 'Maybe now is a good time to offer her an explanation.'

'Can I stay at yours for the night? I don't feel strong

enough to face a barrage of questions.'

To Jeannie's dismay, she saw the colour drain visibly from Jack's face. 'Your mum will want to see you tonight of all nights. I'll give her a ring to let her know you're unwell, but you need to go home.'

Before Jack could reply, a handsome boy in a loose black shirt and tartan trousers ran over to him. 'Found you at last,' he said in an upbeat voice.

The boys' palpable joy at seeing one another gladdened Jeannie's heart.

'This is Tony,' Jack said with love in his eyes.

'I've been looking forward to meeting you,' Jeannie told the exuberant youth.

'Likewise, Jack tells me you're a real dancing queen.'

'I used to be,' Jeannie said with a laugh.

'You're never too old to strut your stuff,' Tony replied. 'You'll have to come clubbing with us sometime.'

His generosity took Jeannie by surprise. 'I need to get back on the horse,' she said to the boys' amusement. 'A night out on the town will do me the world of good.'

Chapter 24

'I love the caramel brown on your tortoiseshell cat,' Jeannie said to Elsie. 'Are you painting any other pets on your coffin?'

'Just a cockapoo on the opposite side. My pets brought me such joy, I'm giving them pride of place.'

'My whippet's my chief companion these days. She follows me around the house like she's afraid of losing me.'

'She probably is, after Frank's death. It makes me sad to think I won't be getting another pet.'

'You've made the right decision; Bella will be my last dog.'

'How did you get on at the evacuee reunion?' Elsie asked as she painted the cat's tail.

'It was interesting, we had a lot to say to one another.'

'I'm not surprised; you shared such precious years together.'

'I discovered I've got a half-brother,' Jeannie said. 'My mum had an illegitimate baby and gave him up for adoption.'

Elsie's eyes widened in surprise. 'What a bombshell,' she said. 'Fancy, your mum and dad not saying a word.'

'They took their secret with them to the grave. The news came as a complete shock to me.'

'Your parents were good people; they must have had their reasons for not keeping the baby.'

'My friend is helping me to find my half-brother, I want to meet him.'

'I'm sure you do. It could be the start of a very special relationship for both of you.'

In a pensive mood, Jeannie dipped a fine brush into the gold paint on her palette. With great care, she painted Frank's name in cursive font on the breast of her coffin. She thought back to the life-defining moment when they first met at the jazz concert. Tired of talking about work to keen young journalists, Frank was sitting by himself on the floor.

Jeannie pictured the men brushing against her at the bar before she flounced away to join him. Thrown together by fate, she recalled her immediate delight at being in Frank's company.

Warm and outgoing, he struck up a meaningful conversation with remarkable ease. 'Everything worth doing carries responsibility,' Frank said in an engaging voice.

Jeannie remembered thinking: 'Did that bloke just say something intelligent to me?' After the crass chat-up lines she'd endured all evening, Frank's authenticity was like a breath of fresh air.

'Don't look now,' Elsie said, 'but Gerald's on his way

over.'

Jeannie sensed immediately that something was wrong. Instead of his usual swagger and overly bright smile, Gerald shuffled towards them with a sad look on his face.

'Is everything alright?' Elsie asked when he reached their table.

Gerald swallowed hard before he spoke: 'I've had to have my horse put down.'

Feeling his pain, Jeannie got up and put her arms around him. 'I'm so sorry,' she said. 'I know how much you loved your horse.'

'Barley kicked the stall door open and broke his leg. I can't believe I'll never ride him again.'

'It's torturous losing an animal, but they live on in our hearts,' Jeannie said.

Gerald grabbed the back of Elsie's chair to steady himself. 'I'll always remember the thrill of seeing Barley galloping in a field with his tail held high.'

'Perhaps, you can paint him on your coffin,' Elsie suggested.

'I tried to do it today, but the pain of losing Barley is still too raw. I'm sorry I'm not my usual cheery self; getting him put down has knocked me for six.'

'Go home and get some rest,' Jeannie advised. 'It will all seem easier tomorrow.'

'Poor man,' Elsie said as Gerald walked away. 'I can't believe he opened up his heart to us.'

'Gerald needed to talk to someone, he's wracked with grief.'

'We certainly saw an unexpected side of him today.'

Jeannie sketched the serene face of a whippet on her coffin as she spoke: 'At last, I'm starting to like the man. I wonder if he'll get another horse?'

Chapter 25

'I'm going clubbing,' Jeannie said as she cleared away her paints.

'Who with?' Elsie asked, raising her eyebrows in surprise.

'My grandson and his boyfriend. It should be a night to remember.'

'Make sure they don't film you dancing and put it on Tik-Tok.'

'My performance days are over, I'm going to the club for a reason,' Jeannie said.

'You can go just to have a good time. It's allowed, you know.'

'I had a great dance at the reunion, but there's some serious sleuthing I want to do in town.'

'Does Jack know what you've got in mind?'

'No, but it concerns him. Last week, he was attacked outside the club and his watch got stolen.'

'It's a crime that's on the increase in the UK,' Elsie said.

'In the last five years, almost 50,000 watches have been stolen. 13% of those thefts included violence.'

'Is Jack alright?' Elsie asked in a worried voice.

'He got badly beaten up, but he was one of the lucky ones. On the same night, a man was stabbed in the heart by a thief stealing his watch.'

'I'm not sure where you come into this,' Elsie said. 'You need to keep well away from violent criminals.'

'They're not the ones I'm going after,' Jeannie told her. 'There's a network of people involved in ensnaring the victims. They pass on vital information to ruthless criminals with alarming frequency.'

'No wonder street robbery is on the increase,' Elsie said.

'Now we're a cashless society, criminals have made luxury watches their currency. Crime lords are experts in watch values, and they use all sorts of tactics to pinpoint their victims.'

'Leave the sleuthing to the experts,' Elsie advised. 'You're talking about organised crime on a serious level.'

'I simply want to feed information to the police,' Jeannie said. 'I have the perfect cover, a night on the town with my grandson. No one would suspect an innocent old lady of collecting vital evidence to catch the Rolex Rippers.'

'Jeannie, I know you like a bit of drama, but this is a step too far,' Elsie cautioned.

'Believe you me, I'll take great care not to attract attention.'

'That's absurd, everyone will notice you. How many people in their 80s will be in the club on the pretext of enjoying modern music?'

'You're not going to get me to change my mind,' Jeannie said. 'The worst thing that can happen is that I end up in my coffin sooner than I intended.'

'That's not even funny,' Elsie snapped. 'Why are you taking such an insane risk?'

'Something Jack said piqued my interest. He seemed to think that the gang were lying in wait for him. As if they'd been given a tip-off that he was wearing a valuable watch.'

'Tell the police, you don't have to get involved.'

'According to my research, organised gangs use "spotters",' Jeannie said. 'Often attractive young women flirt with men in bars and clubs to identify potential victims.'

'I doubt that happened to Jack, he was with his boyfriend,' Elsie commented.

'Exactly, and that's what I want to investigate. Is there a corrupt security guard in the club who identifies people wearing expensive watches? Or a doorman with eagle eyes feeding information to the criminals?'

'Suppose you're right, what do you intend to do about it?' Elsie asked.

'I'll take a few discreet photos and pass them on to the police.'

'Jeannie, they'll have plainclothes officers doing the

exact same thing.'

'Well, they're clearly not doing a very good job, given the number of violent robberies still taking place.'

'Make sure you text me when you get home from the club,' Elsie instructed.

'If you don't hear from me, you'll know I'm in serious trouble,' Jeannie said blithely.

Chapter 26

Jeannie was delighted to learn that a live band was playing at the club. In moments of panic, she'd imagined being squashed to death at a raucous rave revival. Knowing that skilled musicians would be entertaining the crowd allayed her fear.

Determined to look her best, Jeannie fluffed up the roots of her fine pixie-styled hair. She thought of her younger self with long luscious locks, getting ready to go to the Cavern Club. In that era, she'd felt like a resplendent butterfly emerging from a cocoon.

Jeannie pictured herself in a slime-green minidress and gold boots, dancing freely to beat music. 'My halcyon days of youth,' she said as she patted the whippet goodbye.

After so many lonely nights, Jeannie took great pleasure in being in Jack's company. In the aftermath of the attack, he glowed with happiness in the convivial atmosphere of the club.

'Can I get anyone a drink before the band starts playing?' Tony said.

'I feel like stretching my legs, I'll go to the bar,' Jeannie answered.

Unnerved by the boisterous group of people waiting to be served, she hovered in the background. Images of

Jack's badly bruised face flashed into her mind, strengthening her resolve. With a burst of energy, Jeannie doggedly pressed through the crowd to the bar.

Although the bartender taking her order was polite, he was noticeably on edge. His eyes darted manically around the customers whilst the beer flowed against the side of the tilted glass.

At the optimum moment, the bartender gave his full attention to the task at hand. He brought the glass to an upright position and waited until a full, thick head topped the beer.

Jeannie glanced around her to see if anyone was naively wearing an expensive watch. *Nothing to galvanise the Rolex Rippers into action,* she thought as she lifted the drinks from the bar.

Seeing her spill the beer, a young man with strawberry blonde hair stepped forward. 'Let me help you,' he said in a foreign accent Jeannie couldn't place.

What she recognised was the striking image of Van Gogh's *Starry Night* on his shirt. 'Thank you,' she said, 'my hands aren't as steady as they used to be.'

Grateful for the man's assistance, Jeannie pointed out her table in the corner of the room. Walking behind him, she thought of the golden star she'd painted on her coffin in memory of Micky.

Jeannie turned to look at the happy-go-lucky clubbers

dancing with unbridled joy. *In another era it would have all been so different for Micky,*' she told herself.

Jack removed his arm from Tony's shoulder and reached out to take the tray from the man. 'Thanks for helping my grandma,' he said politely.

'It's probably easier if I put the drinks directly on the table,' the man said, stooping down.

Jeannie noticed the sleeve of his shirt ride up over his bronzed arm. To her horror, on his wrist was a luxurious, eye-catching watch. *Take it off before the Rolex Rippers steal it!* she wanted to yell. Instead, she spoke in a calm, steady voice: 'You've been incredibly kind, let me buy you a drink.'

'Absolutely not. It was my pleasure being your knight in shining armour,' the man said.

On high alert, Jeannie watched him edge through the clubbers in the direction of the stage.

'This music's great! Do you fancy a dance, Grandma?' Jack said as he grabbed Tony's hand.

'Not just yet,' Jeannie replied. 'You go and have some fun; I'm happy sitting here.'

Her eyes followed the happy couple onto the dance floor before alighting on the man wearing the watch. In full view of the vigilant doorman, he rolled up his sleeves and leant against the wall.

Chapter 27

The man stayed perfectly still, captivated by the euphoric wave of sound lashing around the room.

Jeannie recognised a hint of psychedelia before the band played a vibrant mix of melodies with mounting energy. The charismatic lead singer rushed to the edge of the stage, grabbing the attention of the crowd.

Staying in detective mode, Jeannie scanned the room for wolfish employers eyeing the watch.

A burly security guard with a forced smile on his face, emerged from the entrance of the club. From his jacket pocket, he whipped out a phone and held it tightly in his tattooed hand.

Her heart racing, Jeannie jumped up from her seat and edged through the fun-loving dancers. Crushed by sweaty bodies, she saw the man waving vigorously to someone across the room. In her mind, his luxurious watch amplified in size, flagging up his presence to the Rolex Rippers.

Confirming her fear, the security guard gaped at the watch like it was a prize trophy being hoisted into the air.

Hell-bent on completing her mission, Jeannie pushed forward to reach the crucial scene.

With cool detachment, the security guard angled his phone camera towards the unsuspecting victim.

From the perfect position, Jeannie snapped the employee doing his dastardly deed. 'Gotcha!' she said triumphantly, under her breath.

Oblivious to the danger he was in, the man walked expectantly towards his female friend.

Jeannie moved to follow him, but a second security guard blocked her path with his hefty body. 'My mate doesn't like having his photo taken,' he said in a sinister voice. 'Give me your phone before he comes over and smashes it to smithereens.'

'He's got nothing to worry about,' Jeannie replied, 'I was photographing my grandson on the dance floor.'

'Don't try to get clever with me,' the man retorted. 'Give me your phone, or I'll crush it in your hand.'

'Here's my grandson,' Jeannie said, pointing to a stranger coming towards her.

The man looked behind him, giving Jeannie a chance to break away. She raced onto the crowded dance floor, desperate to lose the villainous security guards out for her blood.

A lanky lad, flailing his arms around smacked Jeannie in the face, causing her to flinch. Undeterred, she pushed forward into the heart of the crowd to avoid detection.

Elsie's words rang alarmingly in her head: 'Everyone will notice you.' Jeannie wished she could disappear into a magic lamp and be transported out of the club.

When the band stopped playing, a boisterous group of people intent on getting a drink jostled her into the bar area. Jeannie imagined the predatory security guards as gigantic monsters, prowling around the vicinity.

The watchful bartender, scrutinising the clubbers, looked quizzically in her direction. His face contorted into a grimace as he picked up his phone.

Disturbed by the bartender's unnerving stare, Jeannie guessed what he was saying: 'The old crow's standing right in front of me, I'll deal with her now!'

Chapter 28

Jeannie cowered like an animal fearing attack. 'Are you alright?' a woman asked with genuine concern.

'I'm trying to escape from someone,' Jeannie said truthfully.

'Me too, my ex is in the club, and he's the last person I want to see.'

'Do you mind walking me to the door? I'd feel safer with you by my side.'

'I bet that "someone's" a bloke,' the woman remarked. 'Link on to my arm, and if anyone approaches you, I'll kick him where it hurts.'

'You've got it in one! I need to make a getaway before he catches up with me.'

'Don't put up with any male shit,' the woman said. 'Life's for the living.'

Aware that the eagle-eyed bartender was watching her every move, Jeannie clung nervously to the arm of her confidante. Trying to escape the man's gaze, she hastened to the door with her head hung low.

'It's freezing out here,' the woman said when they stepped into the starless night.

'You've been a lifesaver,' Jeannie told her. 'Go back inside and have some fun.'

'Only if you're sure, I can stick around if you want.'

'I'll be fine now. My car's just up the road.'

Jeannie watched the woman walk through the vapers' billowing white smoke into the club.

The lanky bartender stepped into the doorway, wearing a cap pulled down over his eyes.

He strode menacingly down the dimly lit path in Jeannie's direction. *Oh, my God, he's coming to get me. I need to hide the phone!*

She thought of ramming it into the nearest bin, but it was bulging over with takeaway containers. Under immense pressure, a fresh idea ignited in Jeannie's sharpened mind. She pulled out a dog's poo bag from her coat pocket and stuffed the phone inside it.

Her eyes alighted quickly on the red bin under a streetlight, yielding a 'CLEAN IT UP' sticker. Swiftly, Jeannie dropped the phone on top of the pile of dog muck sheathed in plastic bags.

Spotting her Suzuki across the road, she waited for a gap in the whizzing traffic. Just as Jeannie was about to step off the pavement, she felt a tight, painful grip on her arm.

'This is a dangerous place to cross,' the man growled in a vicious voice.

Jeannie tried to wrestle free of his grip, but he was strong and in control.

'Keep on walking, you old bat,' the man commanded.

Jeannie wished she could punch the supercilious moron in the face and knock him to the ground. Instead, the man dug his fist into her back and used his brute strength to push her forward.

'You're wasting your time,' Jeannie told him, 'I haven't got the phone.'

'Then you'll need to tell me where it is before I call my mates.'

'I lost it somewhere in the club.'

'Do you want to be found dead in the middle of the road?' the man said. 'Give me the phone, before I throw you in front of a fast-moving car.'

Jeannie felt the man lift her off the ground, as if he was about to carry out his threat. 'I'll tell you where it is if you let go of me,' she said in a tremulous voice.

'No,' the man snapped. 'You're in my grip until I get my hands on that phone.'

Unable to break free, Jeannie looked back to ascertain the position of her car. In the fading light, she discerned a woman examining the vehicle with acute interest. Wearing clumpy boots, the lady shuffled around the Suzuki like a beady-eyed detective.

'It's Elsie!' Jeannie cried out, making the bartender bristle with rage.

Chapter 29

'Right, down this back alley,' the man said aggressively.

'Elsie,' Jeannie screamed loudly to attract the attention of her Coffin Club ally.

'If that woman tries to intervene, I'll be calling my mates,' the bartender said. 'So shut your mouth.'

Knowing the hyped-up security men were prowling around, Jeannie fell silent. Her stomach in knots, she watched Elsie turn away from the car and march towards the club.

A teenage girl, carrying a football, brushed past Jeannie to cross at the red lights. On the other side of the road, she spoke to Elsie before scooting around a corner.

Although the man's firm hand shoved Jeannie forward, she twisted her head around to look at Elsie.

'Keep on the move, that old hag won't be able to help you,' the man snarled.

To Jeannie's amazement, she got a glimpse of Elsie waving vigorously in her direction.

Buoyed up by the presence of her loyal friend, Jeannie backheeled the man's shin as hard as she could.

'You bitch!' the man shouted out. 'If I don't get that phone, you'll end up with a knife in you.'

Jeannie imagined being stabbed to death in a dark alley before Elsie could reach her. Trying to attract attention to herself, she deliberately tumbled forward and fell to the ground.

A bystander raced to her rescue, but the man stepped in front of him with his hand outstretched. 'My grandma's had too much to drink,' he said in a light-hearted voice, 'leave her to me.'

'They can't take it at her age,' the lad said as he stepped away.

Before Jeannie could speak, the man bent down and smothered her mouth with his weed-stinking hand. 'Death by suffocation, is that what you want?' he said menacingly in her ear.

'Get off my friend,' Elsie hollered, as she stabbed the back of the man's head with a strong, pointy stick.

He turned around, but before he could spring to his feet, Elsie poked the stick into his fiery eyes.

Crying out in agony, the man cowered to the ground like a speared animal.

Elsie quickly pulled a blanket from her bag and threw it over his head. 'Next time, pick on someone your own age,' she told the hoodlum.

'I can't see! I can't see!' the man screamed with a lurch of fright in his voice.

'He looks like a child playing blind man's buff,' Elsie said.

'Come on, Wonder Woman, let's make a run for it,'

Jeannie called out.

Wasting no time, the old pals raced away from the groping villain towards the Suzuki.

When they reached the bright red bin, Jeannie flung up the lid and retrieved the phone secreted in the poo bag.

'I take it that's not dog muck,' Elsie said with a look of incredulity on her face.

'Quick, the man's back on his feet, he'll reach us in no time.'

'There's too much traffic; we can't cross here.'

'The gods are on our side; the lights have changed to red.'

As they charged across the road, the phone in the poo bag started to ring.

'I'll answer that later, when we've made our getaway,' Jeannie said, panting for breath.

Elsie grabbed her friend's hand as she spoke: 'Keep going old girl, you can do it!'

Spurred on by the support, Jeannie forced her tired legs to run as fast as they could.

Safe beside the Suzuki, the women saw the frenzied man dodging fast-moving traffic.

'What a pity, the thug's trapped between whizzing vehicles,' Elsie said with a grin.

To add to his chagrin, Jeannie honked the horn of her car in triumph before pulling away.

Chapter 30

Elsie listened intently to Jeannie's account of her escapades. 'Wow, you've been a busy lady,' she said with a note of admiration in her voice.

'I'll pull into the nearest lay-by and ring Jack,' Jeannie said. 'It was probably him trying to get hold of me earlier.'

'Jack will think you're mad if you tell him the whole story.'

'Someone has to track those villains down; the police are clearly inept.'

'Give them your photos and be done with it. At this rate, we'll both be in our coffins ahead of time.

'Those "spotters" play an insidious role in finding victims for the thieves.'

'I feared they'd catch sight of you, that's why I showed up,' Elsie said.

'What a blessing you did. Without your intervention, that villain might have killed me.'

'Let's just go back to painting our coffins, we might not be so lucky next time.'

'Do me a favour and give the poo bag a wipe,' Jeannie said as she swung into a lay-by.

'It was a stroke of genius hiding the phone in the bin,' Elsie said, as she got to work.

'I surprised myself, it's amazing what a boost of adrenaline does to the old grey cells.'

'Jack's tried several times to get hold of you,' Elsie said, passing the phone to Jeannie.

'He must be wondering where I am, poor lad.'

'It's nice that he's concerned about you, most boys that age are in a world of their own.'

'There are six missed calls,' Jeannie said, furrowing her brow.

'You've been gone a long time; he's keen to locate you.'

'It's more than that, Jack never bombards me with calls.'

Jeannie's finger trembled as she pressed his number. In the foreboding silence, a pervasive tension filled every inch of the car. 'I can't get through, I need to go back to the club,' Jeannie said.

'You'll be placing yourself in great danger if you go back there.'

'I don't care, finding Jack is all that matters.'

'We could swap clothes,' Elsie suggested. 'No one will recognise you in my frumpy skirt and old boots.'

Jeannie spoke over the roar of the engine: 'A disguise would help me slip past the security men.'

'Shall I try Jack's number again?' Elsie asked as Jeannie exited the roundabout.

'Yes, please. It's agony not knowing what's happened to him.'

'Hello,' Elsie said with an intake of breath. 'Sorry, Jeannie, something's wrong with the signal, Jack can't hear me.'

'Thanks for trying. The club's just around the corner, we'll be there soon.'

An ambulance with a loud siren and flashing lights forced Jeannie to pull over onto the verge. With a beating heart, she watched the emergency vehicle drive past at alarming speed.

'The ambulance is stopping outside the club,' Elsie observed.

'Someone needs urgent attention,' Jeannie said with a gasp. 'I hope to God, it's not Jack.'

Chapter 31

Jeannie jumped out of the car and ran fearlessly into the tension-filled club. On the dance floor, a youth was lying in a pool of blood surrounded by busy paramedics.

Determinedly, Jeannie pushed through the clubbers mesmerised by the shocking scene. At the front of the crowd, she spotted the brutish security guard glaring at her with bulging eyes.

In a villainous mood, he stepped forward to block her way with his hefty body.

'I need to find my grandson, please let me pass,' Jeannie pleaded.

'Give me your phone, you old witch,' the man said, baring his teeth.

'Someone stole it from my jacket pocket,' Jeannie told him.

The man grabbed her by the shoulders and gave her a shake. 'Don't play with me,' he said in a low, threatening voice.

'Ouch! You're hurting me,' Jeannie shrieked, attracting the attention of nearby clubbers.

To her great relief, she saw Jack's lithesome figure sprint away from a huddle of police officers. As he came within earshot, he called out forcibly: 'Let go of my grandma.'

Released from the security guard's strong grip, Jeannie ran towards Jack. Up close, the palpable look of terror on his face made her heart lurch. 'Thank heavens you're safe!' she exclaimed, hugging him tightly.

'Tony's been stabbed,' Jack said in an anguished voice. 'We can't get any closer, the paramedics are fighting to save his life.'

Jeannie turned to look at the skilled professionals fixing a tourniquet to Tony's raised arm. Tears welled in her eyes at the sight of the oxygen mask contorting his young face. She saw the bright red blood seeping through the dressing above Tony's heart.

Aware that her legs were wobbling, Jeannie grasped Jack's arm to steady herself.

'They're working as fast as they can to get Tony to hospital,' he said.

Operating with one accord, the paramedics lifted Tony's patched-up body onto the stretcher. Swiftly, they fitted belts across his legs and shoulders before wheeling him out of the club.

Jack's breathing quickened as Tony disappeared from his view. 'Can we follow the ambulance in your car?' he asked.

'Of course,' Jeannie said. 'Have the police contacted Tony's family?'

'Yes. They're making their way to the hospital.'

'His poor family, they'll be torn apart.'

'Tony got stabbed because he kissed me,' Jack cried out in despair.

'A hate crime,' Jeannie said, her voice full of sorrow.

In deathly silence, they hastened past the stunned clubbers to follow the ambulance.

Chapter 32

'Oh, poor Tony!' Elsie exclaimed as she watched him being lifted into the ambulance.

'He might need surgery,' Jeannie said with an intake of breath. 'I'm driving to the hospital with Jack, take yourself home.'

'I tried to get into the club, but that barman was outside having a cigarette. It was too dangerous to pass him.'

'Don't worry about that, you've done enough for tonight.'

'Take care, my lovely. I'll light a candle for that poor boy.'

Jack broke the ongoing silence in the car: 'What was your friend doing outside the club?' he asked.

Jeannie was on the verge of lying to simplify matters. 'She came to check I was alright,' she said after a pause.

Jack paid no heed to her answer. 'It all happened so quickly,' he said. 'One minute Tony was dancing ecstatically, and the next he was on the floor.'

'Have the police got the man who stabbed him?'

'No. He'd disappeared into the crowd before I realised Tony was injured.'

'The incident might have been caught on CCTV.'

'I hope so. If Tony dies, the police will be looking for

a murderer.'

Jeannie followed the swift-moving ambulance down a short driveway to the hospital. 'The Infirmary's got a good reputation, Tony's in the best hands,' she said.

As she pulled into the car park, Jeannie saw the night shrouding the hospital like a sinister black cloak.

'There's a space over there, near the ticket machine,' Jack pointed out.

'It's bloody ridiculous having to pay to park at a hospital,' Jeannie moaned.

'I'll jump out and meet you in A&E,' Jack said as he unfastened his seatbelt.

Traumatised by the mindless stabbing, Jeannie recalled Micky being hurled into the river by Simon. All too vividly, she pictured him slipping under the water, never to be seen again.

If Tony dies, this night will haunt Jack forever, Jeannie thought with a feeling of dread. Alone in the car, she watched her grandson charge through the doors of the busy hospital.

Noting there was a reduced tariff for emergency admissions, Jeannie counted out the coins for the parking metre. *How long will we be in the hospital, awaiting Tony's fate?* she wondered as she fed the money into the machine.

The long line of ambulances queuing up outside A&E

made Jeannie's heart pound. *Tony's in a critical state, a delay could cost him his life,* she told herself.

Inside the hospital, Jack was slumped dejectedly against a wall, like a wounded animal.

Fearing the worst, Jeannie ran quickly to his side. 'Have you had any news?' she asked calmly.

'No, Tony's still in the ambulance. His parents are on their way.'

Jeannie grasped Jack's shaking body in her arms to mollify his terror.

'Tony might already be dead,' he said mournfully.

The wretched sound of Jack's sobbing brought tears to Jeannie's eyes. She stroked the back of his sweat-sodden head as she spoke: 'Once Tony has been admitted, the trauma team will spring into action. All we can do is wait and pray.'

Chapter 33

'Tony got stabbed to death in the club,' Jeannie told Ruth over the telephone. 'Jack's in a dreadful state.'

'Oh my God, that's appalling news.'

'Jack's going to stay at my house tonight.'

'Why doesn't he want to come home?'

'Jack's torn apart, sweetheart, it doesn't matter where he sleeps.'

'It does to me,' Ruth said. 'He's my boy and I want to see him.'

Jeannie looked at Jack rocking backwards and forwards in lacerating pain. 'Tony's parents are distraught,' she said, 'they've lost their only child.'

'I feel for them,' Ruth replied. 'Tony was such a beautiful free spirit.'

Her words went straight to Jeannie's heart. 'It's history repeating itself,' she said wistfully.

'Mum, are you alright?' Ruth asked. 'It's been an agonising night for you and Jack.'

'I'm trying to be strong, but I don't feel very well.'

'Don't get in the car, I'll drive to the hospital and pick you up.'

'Thanks, you're a real life-saver,' Jeannie said.

'Just sit in a chair and wait until I get there. I won't be long.'

By the time Ruth entered the hospital, Jeannie was asleep in Jack's arms like a slumbering child.

'Grandma fainted, for a moment I thought she was dead,' Jack said in a quavering voice.

'Oh, darling, it's devastating news about Tony. You must be in total shock.'

'Who stabs someone because they're gay?' Jack asked, his face contorted with grief.

'A madman,' Ruth said, giving him a warm embrace.

The shift in Jack's body caused Jeannie to open her eyes. 'Where am I?' she asked in a state of bewilderment.

'We're at the hospital,' Jack said, making her gasp in sadness.

'Why don't you stay at mine for the night?' Ruth suggested. 'I'll take care of you both.'

'You'll nag me about Dad,' Jack blurted out. 'I can't take any more of your aggro.'

Ruth grimaced at his honest retort. 'Ryan's the last thing on my mind, you're the only one who matters.'

Jeannie touched her daughter lightly on the shoulder. 'I'd like to stay at yours tonight if that's alright with Jack,' she said.

'Whatever you want, Grandma, I'm not in the mood to fight. Tony's lying dead in this hospital, and I feel like joining him.'

Anguished by Jack's remark, Jeannie and Ruth lifted

him gently from the seat. Their arms linked together, they walked out of the hospital into the cold dark night.

Chapter 34

'There was a real outpouring of love for Tony at his funeral,' Jeannie told Elsie at the Coffin Club. 'He was clearly adored by everyone who knew him.'

'Poor Jack, the day must have been harrowing for him.'

'His fortitude was remarkable. He managed to recite a poem for Tony in a tender, uplifting voice.'

'I don't know where he got his strength from, I was a wreck at Billy's funeral.'

'"Rest in power, my soulmate," Jack said when he touched Tony's coffin.'

'I've been reading about hate crime, I didn't realise it was such a big issue,' Elsie remarked.

'There's been a 41% increase in homophobic attacks in the last year,' Jeannie said.

'The toxic language used by some politicians doesn't help matters.'

'Gay people live in a perpetual state of fear, but they won't be silenced. The LGBTQ+ community sent Jack amazing messages of support.'

'That's wonderful, their love and understanding will mean a lot to him.'

'All gay people want is freedom to be themselves and live their lives to the full.'

'That's not too much to ask in a civilised society,' Elsie said.

'It's a strange world we live in, but the LGBTQ+ community is a strong, powerful force. They will turn the tide against the violence.'

'I hope so, for our children's sake. Who wants them to be stabbed to death for expressing their love?'

'Tony's death has touched the hearts of many people. He'll be remembered for living his truth.'

'Which hopefully will inspire others to do the same,' Elsie replied.

'All the sixth formers wore rainbow-coloured t-shirts to the funeral,' Jeannie said. 'There was a blaze of energy in the church.'

'A surge of love to celebrate Tony's short life.'

'The front of the altar was adorned with pure white roses.'

'A glorious funeral after that horrific stabbing.'

'My heart aches for Jack, he will never forget that awful night.'

'Did you hand your photos to the police?' Elsie asked, remembering their escapade.

'I did, but they didn't seem interested. When the police were dealing with Tony's stabbing, the officers were fantastic. They acted extremely quickly - interviewing people, watching the CCTV cameras.'

'Have they arrested someone for Tony's murder?'

'Yes, a man in his 30s. He openly admitted it was a hate crime.'

'Why did the police dismiss the photos of the "spotter" in the club?'

'Who knows? It was like they were turning a blind eye to watch theft. I suspect some corrupt officers are getting a backhander.'

Elsie nudged Jeannie gently on the elbow. 'Gerald looks a lot happier,' she said, as he strode jauntily towards them.

'I bet he's got himself a new horse,' Jeannie whispered.

'I've bought myself a Thoroughbred to liven up my old age,' Gerald announced when he reached their table.

'Good for you,' Jeannie said. 'Life's precious, we've all got to make the most of it.'

Chapter 35

In the afternoon sunshine, Jeannie sat alone, admiring Frank's carefully planned garden. Just as he intended, the bright red poppies looked resplendent against the dry stone wall. Equally arresting, yellow begonias circled the apple tree like merry dancers. Even the withering brown flowers past their best retained a bedraggled beauty.

'There you are,' Ruth called out from the kitchen doorway. 'I thought I might find you in the garden.'

'It's where I feel closest to your father,' Jeannie said. 'He put his heart and soul into creating this haven.'

'Dad had green fingers; the garden looks beautiful. I just wish I had more time to enjoy it.'

'"What is this life if full of care, we have no time to stand and stare?"[4]' Jeannie said cheerfully.

'You've forgotten what it's like holding down a full-time job, with management breathing down your neck,' Ruth retorted.

'All the more reason to take pleasure in little things.'

'Your prescription's on the kitchen table, sorry I can't stop,' Ruth said. 'I've got an important meeting at two o'clock.'

'Sit down, you're entitled to a lunch break,' Jeannie

---

[4] W.H Davies, *Leisure,* first published in 1911 by A.C Fifield.

replied.

Ruth tutted in exasperation. 'I'm a full-time working parent struggling to do my job, relaxing in the garden isn't my priority.'

'You don't seem happy at the moment,' Jeannie said with concern in her voice.

'Of course, I'm not! Jack's on the verge of a breakdown, and Ryan's back on the scene.'

'It's a very difficult time,' Jeannie said, 'Jack needs the support of his father.'

'Not one who walked out on me when I had postnatal depression.'

'Ryan left the family home because he was afraid of hurting Jack.'

'He abandoned me and his newborn son without any warning.'

'Ryan should have got treatment earlier, but he was ashamed of having postnatal depression.'

'I was his wife, for heaven's sake, he had no right to keep me in the dark.'

'Ryan was afraid of losing you if he told you the truth.'

'So instead, he just walks out the door like a coward.'

'Ryan had no choice; he'd been referred to hospital.'

'There you go again, seeing everything from his point of view.'

'I'm only pointing out the facts,' Jeannie said calmly. 'At the time, you were both ill and struggling to cope.'

'Ryan will be a bad influence on Jack,' Ruth said. 'The man's got no backbone.'

'It looks like Ryan's here to stay this time. You need to talk to him, for Jack's sake.'

Ruth collapsed into a chair with tears in her eyes. 'Why is life so fucking hard?' she asked in a dejected voice.

Jeannie wrapped her arms around her sobbing daughter. 'Let me make you some lunch whilst you relax in the garden,' she said.

Chapter 36

'Let's have our picnic down by the river,' Jeannie said to Jack.

'Thanks for picking me up, Grandma, I was desperate to get out of the house. Mum's been watching my every move like I'm a patient in intensive care.'

'She's naturally worried about you, her behaviour's perfectly normal.'

'At least she's spoken to my dad and accepted that he's part of my life.'

'I'm pleased about that, the way they separated broke my heart.'

'I should have told Mum that we'd met up; it would have been easier in the long run.'

'Your dad is a lovely man; I'm not surprised you get on.'

'It's more than that; until I met him, I felt like part of me was missing.'

Jeannie recalled Ethan saying the exact same thing when she visited him in the Forest of Dean. 'Was it you who first made contact with Ryan?' she asked gently.

'Yes, his name is on my birth certificate, it wasn't hard to track him down.'

Jeannie squeezed Jack's hand as she spoke: 'What a joy, finding your father.'

'I feel more complete since I met my dad,' Jack replied.

'It's strange that Ryan was living so close by, I thought he'd moved to Spain.'

'His home is in Sitges, but he's bought a flat near my grandad.'

Although Jack was talking about his paternal grandfather, Jeannie pictured Frank. She saw him fishing on the bank of the river with his beloved grandson by his side. 'It's wonderful you have a new family to love and cherish you,' she said.

In a contemplative frame of mind, Jeannie looked out at the countryside saturated in colour. 'I always think of Vincent Van Gogh when I see a golden field of corn,' she remarked. 'No artist captured its ravishing beauty with such force.'

'He wouldn't leave Arles when the wheat fields were in full bloom,' Jack said.

'It's an inspiring sight for an artist attuned to nature.'

'Tony read Vincent's letters aloud to me, they were incredibly moving.'

'Your mum told me that Tony's parents have given you all his books.'

'They have; it's been emotional looking through them. I can feel Tony peering over my shoulder when I read his scrappy marginalia.'

'Those we love never truly leave us,' Jeannie said.

'How are you coping without Grandad?' Jack asked. 'He was such a huge part of our lives.'

'Oh, he makes an appearance every day,' Jeannie answered. 'He keeps reminding me to get back on the horse.'

'Well, don't get galloping away, I need you by my side,' Jack said, taking Jeannie's arm.

'I won't be going far, sweetheart, everything I treasure is right on my doorstep.'

Happy in each other's company, Jeannie and Jack walked in silence down to the glistening river.

Chapter 37

Breathing deeply at the red lights, Jeannie glanced over to the garish Vape Shop. The neon purple lights made it look like a seedy brothel touting for punters. Although the lights changed to red and amber, Jeannie fixated on the furtive-looking men in the doorway.

Recognising the lanky bartender from the club, she tried to place the red-headed man sidling up to him. *A shady drug deal*, Jeannie thought as the blast of a horn impelled her to drive on.

Something about the short man's grimace seemed disturbingly familiar to Jeannie. When she remembered where she'd seen the moron, she swung into a parking bay with surprising ease. *It's the arrogant policeman who fobbed me off at the station. I was right, he didn't want photos of the 'spotters' because he's in on the act.*

Jeannie thought of Jack being attacked outside the club, a week after the Rolex Rippers carried out a fatal stabbing. *A murder ignored by corrupt police officers aiding and abetting crime.*

She jumped out of the car and, without paying for a parking ticket, ran towards the Vape Shop. Seeing the policeman and bartender deep in conversation, Jeannie positioned herself behind a parked lorry.

Her heart beating fast, she reached for her phone to

record their criminal activity.

The bartender looked around him before producing a wad of cash from his jacket pocket.

With a shaky hand, Jeannie zoomed in on the action with her phone camera. Stealthily, she waited for the policeman to grasp the money before taking her shot. 'Got you bastards,' she whispered in triumph.

The roar of an engine alerted Jeannie to the fact that the lorry was reversing towards her. In the nick of time, she leapt onto the pavement away from the advancing vehicle.

Disturbed by the beeping from the lorry, the men simultaneously turned their heads around.

'It's fucking Miss Marple,' the bartender called out in a vicious tone.

'Grab her!' the policeman instructed. 'The devious old cow's onto us.'

In her effort to escape, Jeannie tripped over a cracked slab and fell hard to the ground.

The lanky barman sprinted towards her like a Good Samaritan intent on rescue.

Anxious to secrete her phone, Jeannie pushed it deep into her bag before scrabbling to her knees. With her bloody hand, she waved frantically to the lorry driver looking in his mirror.

He was halfway out of his cab when the thuggish

bartender hauled Jeannie to her feet.

Keeping alert, she looked at the address on the side of the lorry. 'I feel too dizzy to drive. Are you going anywhere near Aigburth?' she called out to the driver.

'Well, there's a coincidence,' the man remarked. 'That's my next stop.' With two chubby hands, he hitched up his baggy trousers and reached for Jeannie's bag.

Raging with fury, the bartender grabbed it first. 'No worries, mate, I can give her a lift,' he snapped.

'I've always wanted a ride in a lorry, it's on my bucket list,' Jeannie said sweetly.

Riled by the slimy bartender, the driver yanked the bag out of his hand. 'The lady wishes to travel by lorry,' he said, emulating a posh voice.

The driver opened the passenger door and graciously helped Jeannie ascend the step.

Safe in the cab, she watched the bartender race back to his ally, lurking in the shadows. *Your days are numbered, I'll make sure you evil criminals are brought to justice,* Jeannie pledged.

Chapter 38

Jeannie watched Elsie take a porcelain figurine from the shelf and wrap it in newspaper. 'You're brave downsizing,' she said, 'I don't have the strength to do it.'

'It's too difficult for me running a house this size,' Elsie replied. 'With the heating bills being so high, I can't afford the repairs.'

'Flying solo's hard,' Jeannie said. 'I took for granted how much Frank did to keep us afloat.'

'Although I'll miss the garden, it will be a relief moving into a flat.'

'I considered downsizing, but the thought of leaving my home tears me apart.'

'When the time is right to find a new place, you'll get the wind in your sails.'

'I'm not sure about that, but I am going abroad with my family. Ryan's letting us use his house in Sitges for a couple of weeks.'

'A break will do you good after your tussle with the police.'

'It's going to be a long ride bringing those villains to justice.'

'At least they're behind bars now, thanks to you. It was a brainwave taking your photos to the press.'

'The reporters were already doing an investigation into

the Rolex Rippers. Given the lack of prosecutions, they suspected police corruption.'

'Without your intervention, the criminals would have gotten away with it for a lot longer.'

'You're right,' Jeannie said. 'The police were identifying the undercover officers to the gang.'

'Then you show up and outwit them all.'

'I got the photos at the right time; they helped the reporters nail their exposé.'

'And you say I'm brave. You're the most courageous person I know.'

'Frank will be pleased I'm not fading away,' Jeannie said.

'Just the opposite, I'd say. I don't know where you get your energy from.'

'After Tony's life was cut short, I've come to appreciate the blessing of old age.'

'Because of the war, my dad valued every precious day of his long life.'

'He was a great one for keeping up his spirits. My father was prone to mood swings.'

Elsie stopped wrapping her ornaments and looked Jeannie in the eye. 'It's marvellous that you've made contact with your half-brother,' she said.

'I got very emotional when I spoke to Charlie. Knowing he was my mum's love child, and she had to put him up for adoption, filled me with sadness.'

'Have you planned to meet up with him?'

'Yes, Charlie's coming to visit me in the autumn. It will be wonderful seeing my mother's son.'

'She'll be dancing in heaven knowing you've found one another.'

Jeannie gave a broad, sunshiny smile. 'Do you want me to stay and help with the packing?' she said. 'It's a lot for you to do on your own.'

'Gerald's coming over later, he's going to give me a hand.'

'I didn't know you spoke to him outside the Coffin Club,' Jeannie said, raising her eyebrows.

'I made friends with Gerald on Facebook. He's been sending me photos of his beautiful horse.'

'That's surprising, I didn't have him down as the sharing type.'

'Gerald makes an effort to brighten my day. I'm looking forward to his visit.'

'Well, good for you, companionship staves off loneliness.'

'Old friends are the best for doing that,' Elsie said. 'Make sure you stay safe; I couldn't bear to lose you.'

Jeannie slipped on her jacket as she spoke: 'Now those criminals are locked away, my sleuthing days are over.'

'That's a relief, I don't fancy fighting off any more

murderous thugs.'

Jeannie gave Elsie a big hug. 'No more fraternising with society's underbelly, I promise you. This time next week, I'll be basking in the glorious Spanish sunshine.'

Jeannie flapped around in the sea like a playful child before plunging deep into the water. White glistening waves tickled her face as she swam gently away from the shoreline.

Entranced by the incredible blueness of the sky, 'This is heaven on earth,' she called out to Frank. 'Come and join me.'

Feeling his closeness, Jeannie synched into the rhythm of his strong strokes. Like ageless water babies, they swam side by side in the peaceful, undulating water.

'We've gone far enough,' Jeannie heard Frank say. 'It's time for you to turn back now.'

Lost in bliss, Jeannie swam further and further towards the celestial horizon.

'Don't try to follow me,' Frank said. 'Jack's waiting for you on the beach.'

The thought of her adored grandson anticipating her return impelled Jeannie to turn around.

From the water's edge, the colourful towels strewn across the beach looked like strips of candy. Squinting in the bright sunshine, Jeannie scanned the golden sands in search of Jack. All around, male couples were openly displaying their affection with comfortable ease. Jeannie groaned inwardly. *Being in this gay haven will intensify Jack's pain at losing Tony. I should never have brought him to Sitges.*

She recalled the fateful night Tony got stabbed in the club for kissing Jack. *A senseless act of violence against a gay man in the prime of his life.*

Sighting Jack's orange sun umbrella, Jeannie raced over the scorching sand to be with him. Up close, she saw a book entitled 'Grief is a Thing with Feathers' lying face down on his sun bed.

Jeannie glanced over to the bar, hoping to see Jack straddled on a stool with a beer in his hand. An elderly man with a leering expression on his face gave her a vigorous wave. Embarrassed, she turned away and rummaged in her capacious beach bag for a towel.

Awkwardly peeling off her wet swimsuit next to an amorous couple, Jeannie yearned for Frank's company. Being miles from home without her attentive soulmate, she felt like she'd severed a limb.

'You need to find Jack,' Frank said in a gentle, persuasive voice.

Realising that she'd put her dress on inside out, Jeannie let out a long, deep sigh. *Calm down,* she told herself. *Jack's not in any danger; he's going to be fine.*

As she was pulling the dress over her head, Jeannie heard the muffled sound of her phone ringing. By the time she located her mobile under her straw hat, Jack had left a message.

Greatly relieved that he'd made contact, Jeannie listened intently to his voice:

'Hi, Grandma, I went for a walk to process what happened with my mum. I'm sitting on the rocks near the church if you want to join me.'

Jeannie hastened along the promenade, smiling at the male couples proudly pushing their baby strollers. In light of Jack's message, she thought about Ruth's excuse for not coming to Sitges. *Being too busy at work doesn't ring true. I need to hear from Jack the real reason Ruth stayed at home.*

Chapter 40

Jeannie looked in awe at the dramatic baroque church gracing the skyline. In her eyes, the splendid polygonal tower topped with a belfry added grandeur to the landmark.

Impressed by the busker playing his guitar at the foot of the church steps, Jeannie dropped a coin in his hat. The musician's sunshiny demeanour reminded her of Jack before he lost Tony.

She turned towards the outcrop of rocks running down to the sea. Jack was seated alone, staring into the depths of the lapping water.

Jeannie called out his name, but he remained inert, oblivious to her presence. Determined to reach him, Jeannie stepped cautiously over the rocks in her flimsy sandals.

Even when Jack knew she was beside him, he stayed fixated on the deep blue ocean.

Jeannie put her arms around him as she spoke, 'What an idyllic spot for watching the waves.'

'Tony would have loved it here in Sitges,' Jack said.

'I was worried it would make you sad seeing all the openly gay couples.'

'It only brings me joy, Grandma. Imagine if everywhere in the world was like Sitges.'

'You're being very brave. It must be agony being here without Tony.'

'Being without him is painful wherever I am. Sitges is a wonderful place for the LGBTQ+ community.'

'Did you go into the beautiful church?' Jeannie asked.

'No. Children were preparing for their First Holy Communion, so I came to the rocks.'

'A perfect place to process what happened with your mum.'

'We had the most awful row after I found my dad's presents,' Jack said.

Taken aback, Jeannie winced at the pain in his voice.

'I was looking for my Spanish dictionary in the attic when I discovered them. A boxful of unopened gifts from my dad, addressed to me.'

'Your mother was unwell when she hid them away, she was incapable of thinking straight.'

'Everything has always been centred around her,' Jack said. 'She made me think my dad didn't want to know me.'

'Your mother's illness made her denigrate your father. He's found it in his heart to forgive her, you need to do the same.'

'I read my dad's cards telling me how much he loved me. If I hadn't gone searching for him, we might never have met.'

Jeannie thought of her secret half-brother put up for adoption. 'It's miraculous that you've been reunited with your dad after all these years,' she said.

'I'm pleased Mum didn't come on holiday; I needed to get away from her.'

'She blocked your father out of her life to survive. Try to understand things from her point of view.'

'Finding those carefully wrapped presents broke my heart,' Jack said.

'You've discovered you've got two loving parents, see it as a blessing.'

'That's easy for you to say, no one's ever deliberately kept you in the dark.'

Jeannie placed her hand over Jack's clenched fist. 'Sometimes people inflict pain on those they love the most,' she told him. 'It's a tragic fact of life.'

Chapter 41

Jeannie's elation at seeing the treasure trove of family photos was riddled with guilt. *I haven't looked at these since we cleared Mum's house many moons ago*, she said to herself. *They're far too precious to be boxed away out of sight.*

With Charlie's visit in mind, Jeannie searched for notable images of her mother to show him. In one striking photo, four immaculate women in WVS uniforms had their arms around one another. Glowing with pride, Jeannie recognised her pretty, elegant mother third from the right. *Even in a plain, mid-length dress with three patch pockets, she exudes style and sophistication*, Jeannie thought.

When she pulled an old newspaper from the box, the whippet barked as if initiating conversation. 'It's just wartime memorabilia, you silly girl,' Jeannie said as she examined her find.

The shocking images of the devastation brought to Bristol during the air raids made her gasp. Distraught people, streaked in blood, clung together beside a burned-out bus. Cherished historic buildings in the heart of the city were smashed to rubble.

'1,299 people were killed in the Bristol Blitz,' Jeannie read before turning over the page.

Her mother looked radiant in the main press photo

illustrating the feature. Dressed in her WVS uniform, she was standing next to a stretcher-bearer with a broad smile on her face. Something about their proximity to one another suggested to Jeannie that they were in a relationship.

Thinking she might have identified Charlie's father, she read the feature with intense interest. It reported that her mother's canteen provided food to the stretcher parties carrying wounded soldiers from the railway station.

A chance for love to flourish, Jeannie told herself. *Or, maybe, the man was my mum's ex-boyfriend, and their relationship got rekindled.*

Before she could speculate further, the whippet leapt into the windowsill to bark at the postman.

Charlie's birth must have been such a shock for my dad, Jeannie thought as she stepped over to the dog. Stroking the whippet, she looked out at the rich profusion of cherry blossoms hanging from the tree.

'Oh, Frank, all I know for sure is that I loved my mother with all my heart,' Jeannie told him.

The cream letter in beautiful handwriting lifted her spirits until she realised who it was from. *Why would Simon send me a letter?* Jeannie asked herself as she perched on the sofa.

Despite the passage of time, her memory of him hurling Micky into the river was vividly real.

Dearest Jeannie, she read,

I hope you are well and thriving in your retirement.

My cancer diagnosis has compelled me to write to you about that fateful summer in the Forest of Dean. I desperately need your forgiveness for the heinous wrong I did to Micky.

Please don't see me as a murderer, I was a spiteful, ignorant child who did a terrible thing. When Micky was dancing around in your dress, it triggered something in me. I've spent a lifetime regretting my impulsive fit of rage which led to his death.

Although I've tried to lead a good life and atone for my wicked deed, the moment Micky slipped under the water still torments me. I'm afraid to meet my maker because I fear I have blood on my hands.

Micky was a beautiful, free spirit who had the misfortune to encounter a mindless bully. In my dreams, I imagine dancing with him beside the river, happy and carefree.

Please find it in your heart to forgive my childish cruelty, Jeannie. Only with your understanding, will I be able to rest in peace.

All my love,
Simon.

Hearing Jeannie sob, the attentive whippet jumped onto the sofa to comfort her.

Chapter 42

Jeannie doodled on her writing pad whilst collecting her thoughts. She recalled the children in *Blue Remembered Hills* who, in high spirits, locked Donald in the barn. *Theirs was a rash prank that went wrong,* she told herself. *Simon hurled Micky into the river intending to punish him.*

Jeannie pictured the horror and panic on Simon's face when he failed to rescue Micky from the water. *Just as the children fought to save Donald from the burning barn, Simon tried to pull Micky from the depths of the river,* she conceded.

It distressed her to think that she'd called Simon a murderer at the reunion. Wanting to assuage his pain, Jeannie began writing the letter he yearned for.

Dear Simon, she wrote,

Thank you for getting in touch at this difficult time in your life. I hope you respond well to your cancer treatment and make a full recovery.

Your letter, addressing the circumstances of Micky's death, made a great impact on me. It took enormous courage for you to revisit the past with such honesty.

I'm not going to do you a disservice by fabricating the

facts of Micky's death. You threw him into the river in a fit of rage because he was wearing my dress. I was there, I saw it with my own eyes and, for all those years, I thought you'd murdered my sweet friend.

What I chose to forget was how desperately hard you fought to rescue Micky. You wanted him to live. I saw the palpable agony on your face when you emerged from the river without him.

Taking this into account, I ask your forgiveness for my deliberate blindness and lack of compassion. You can rest in peace, knowing that your childish rage was superseded by a brave effort to save Micky.

I hope my letter lifts a weight from your troubled mind, dear friend. If you are at the reunion next year, we'll dance together in remembrance of Micky.

All my love,
Jeannie

After the effort of writing, Jeannie closed her eyes in a moment of tranquillity. Lost in thought, she paid no heed to Jack entering the room.

'Hi, Grandma, are you okay?' Jack asked in a concerned voice.

Slightly startled, Jeannie took a moment to respond. 'I am,' she said eventually. 'Is everything alright at home?'

'I haven't run away if that's what you mean. I've brought you some Italian chocolates to say thanks for an amazing holiday.'

Jeannie took the prettily wrapped box from Jack's outstretched hand. 'That's very kind of you,' she said. 'They're my favourites.'

'Mum said they were.'

'How are things between the two of you?'

'Better, now we've talked about her postnatal depression.'

'When your mum was at her worst, she wouldn't go outside, in case you got attacked by a dog.'

'She explained to me how postnatal depression took away her sense of reality.'

'Have you forgiven your mum for hiding the presents and cards?'

'Yes, she just couldn't confront the awfulness of the past.'

'It was tragic that your parents got postnatal depression at the same time. Your dad left because he was fearful of hurting you.'

'When he got better, Mum was afraid to have him back in the house.'

'In the end, it was easier for them to separate.'

'I don't think it was,' Jack said. 'The split tore them both apart.'

'Your mum should have been open with you about the past.'

'That's what I thought until she disclosed the impact of her postnatal depression.'

'I'm immensely proud of you,' Jeannie said. 'It takes strength to step into someone else's shoes and see their point of view.'

Determined to display the tulips in all their glory, Jeannie arranged them carefully in the vase. Delighted with her artistry, she placed the flowers next to Frank's photograph on the piano.

Illuminated by a beam of light, his twinkly eyes seemed to be watching her every move. 'Imagine a horse galloping through a beautiful meadow, feel that life force running through you,' Jeannie heard him say.

Buoyed on by Frank's mantra, she walked jauntily into the kitchen to check on the quiche. Crisp and golden brown, it reminded her of the delicious tarts her mother used to bake. *What a pity she's not here to meet her son*, Jeannie thought. *Being reunited with Charlie would have brought her such joy.*

At that moment, Jeannie sensed the presence of her mother in the kitchen. She pictured her with outstretched arms eagerly waiting to embrace her son.

Picking up on the atmosphere, the whippet stared at her mistress with wide-open eyes.

'You're going into the living room, I don't want you stealing the quiche,' Jeannie told the dog.

Through the window, she saw a pretty girl with blonde curly hair, waving from a car. Tall and slim like their mother, Charlie alighted from the vehicle and lifted the child out of her seat.

Bursting with excitement, Jeannie raced down the driveway to greet her family.

'Charlie,' she cried out, as she gave her half-brother a mighty hug.

'Jeannie, it's wonderful to see you,' he said, tears streaming down his face.

The vivacious girl ran over to see the howling whippet, perched in the window.

Jeannie looked intently at the captivating child. *My mother's great-granddaughter,* she thought with a warm sense of love.

'Celeste adores dogs, especially ones that give her a lot of fuss,' Charlie said.

Jeannie remembered Rita's whippet, jumping up to lick her face when she arrived in the Forest of Dean. 'It gladdens my heart to have a little girl in the house,' she told Charlie.

'Celeste is intrigued by your sudden appearance in our lives. She calls you "Magic Jeannie" as if you've come out of a bottle.'

'Everything's so delightful through the eyes of a child. I want you both to feel at home here.'

As soon as Jeannie pushed open the door, Celeste bounded into the house in search of the dog.

Charlie put his suitcase down in the hallway and took

Jeannie's hands. 'It feels like a miracle, finding you so late in my life,' he said.

Elated to be united with her half-brother, Jeannie felt the power of the Wind Horse surging through her. 'Together, we're moving on to rich new pastures,' she said in a jubilant voice.

Chapter 44

'Mum was beautiful,' Charlie said, as he perused the photograph in the newspaper. 'Ever likely my dad fell in love with her.'

'Even on duty, in their uniform, they look like a couple in love,' Jeannie remarked.

'Although I never met my parents, I feel a strong affinity with them.'

'It is deeply sad that they had to put you up for adoption.'

'When your father came back from the war, he was a broken man. Mum was duty-bound to put him first,' Charlie said.

'It pains me to think I knew nothing about your existence.'

'Learning that your mother had an illegitimate child must have come as a great shock to you. The way you have reached out to me has touched my heart.'

'Having you in my life is a great blessing,' Jeannie said. 'Mum was a remarkable woman, her relationship with your dad mystifies me.'

'Dad bequeathed me the last letter she wrote to him,' Charlie said, reaching into his jacket pocket. 'It's deeply distressing, but it sheds a lot of light on my parents' love for one another.'

'Will you read it to me?' Jeannie said. 'All her life, Mum poured her heart and soul into her letter writing. I know it will be a powerful account of her truth.'

Charlie placed the letter on his lap and straightened it out with his bony hand.

Full of anticipation, Jeannie closed her eyes to hear the longed-for disclosure of her mother's story.

My darling Edward, Charlie read,

Our baby has gone. My heart aches for all three of us, we will never be together again.

The sound of Charlie screaming when I left him will haunt me forever. We have paid too big a price for loving one another, Edward.

Oh, why did you visit the canteen on that fateful day and re-enter my life?

When you were injured in the bombing, I was distraught that I would lose you all over again. Nursing you back to health lit a fire in me that I could not extinguish.

Years ago, a bigoted priest poisoned my parents' minds with his dogma. They tore me away from you because you were not a Catholic boy.

Know always that my love for you and our darling son will not be broken. You both will live on in my heart because you are part of me.

Forgive me for the decisions I have made, but I am duty-bound to stay with my husband.

Jeannie, my adorable daughter, will be home soon to lighten my load. Without her, I wouldn't have the strength to go forward in life.

I'm sorry that my tears have blotted the ink on this pitiful letter. Letting you go is making me ill with sorrow.

From the depths of my soul, I love you and Charlie. I will think of you both every day until I die.

Yours forever,
Rose

Caught between worlds, Jeannie imagined she was rocking her mother gently in her arms. 'It's alright, Mum,' she said. 'Charlie's here with me and your beautiful great-granddaughter is asleep upstairs.'

A lightbulb flickering in the chandelier brought Jeannie back to reality. 'What a poignant letter,' she heard Charlie say.

Jeannie smiled at her teary half-brother as she spoke: 'It's a heartfelt testimony of Mum's deep love for you and your dad.'

'Her story tears me apart. I can't believe Mum encountered so many twists and turns of fate.'

'Life's a rich tapestry of sorrow and joy for us all,' Jeannie said. 'Despite being wracked with pain, Mum showered me with love when I returned home.'

'She was a spirited woman; I feel blessed to have discovered her story.'

'Mum rode the Wind Horse through the storm and galloped on with her head held high. Her courage is a great inspiration to us all,' Jeannie said proudly.

End

About The Author

Jacky Warwicker is a retired drama/performing arts teacher, living in North East England.

Through writing, she has discovered a new way of communicating with an audience. Her stories illuminate the courage of people scrambling through upending change. Using varied settings and compelling voices of all ages, they champion the importance of human connection.

In 2023 her debut anthology of short stories, *Journey's Bend*, was published – a mixture of genres, the creative tales twist and turn through the vagaries of life.

This was followed in 2024 by the publication of her first novella, *In Every Season*, which celebrates the enduring power of love.

Her latest, emotionally packed novella, *Moving On*, weaves together heroic stories across four generations.

In addition to exploring places of cultural interest, Jacky enjoys going to the theatre and hiking.

www.blossomspringpublishing.com

www.ingramcontent.com/pod-product-compliance
Lightning Source LLC
Chambersburg PA
CBHW052138170626
46812CB00004B/1494